# Loving Au

## Book Two (The Se

# By
# Lilly Adam

ISBN:9798531499868

*Dedicated to my wonderful readers; I hope you enjoy reading this book as much as I enjoyed writing it.*

When you are old and grey and full of
sleep,
And nodding by the fire, take down this
book,
And slowly read, and dream of the soft
look
Your eyes had once, and of their shadows
deep;
**William Butler Yeats**

Storyteller at Heart

## Also written by Lilly Adam:

May of Ashley Green
Stella
Poppy Woods
The Whipple Girl
Rose
Whitechapel Lass
Daisy Grey
Beneath the Apple Blossom Tree
Faye
Secrets of the Gatehouse
Searching for Eleanor (Book one)

# CHAPTER ONE
September 1878

As she leaned against the heavily laced window, Eleanor couldn't wait for August's arrival to Paradise Street; she was bursting to announce her exciting news to him. It had been a week ago, on the previous Sunday when she'd spent the day with him in East Hanwell; a day which had ended in a heated discussion as to where they would live after their marriage, due to take place at the end of October. Her grandmother was set on them living in the tiny hamlet; after being separated from Eleanor for all of her life, she trembled with fear at the very thought of being so far away from her again, even though August had promised that they'd visit every Sunday. But in her wisdom she spoke of the many obstacles which could easily put an end to such future visits; bad weather, illness, and then, when the babies began to arrive, she had declared, turning both August and Eleanor's cheeks a shade of scarlet, the visits would only prove an inconvenience. In August's opinion, Prudence Whitlock was looking far too deep into the future and causing more problems than they needed at such a thrilling period of his and Eleanor's life. He'd waited too long for this special moment which had often been overshadowed by a heavily weighted notion that

Eleanor was gone from his life forever. From now on he wanted everything in their life to be perfect, and as he and Eleanor strove to keep everyone happy it was proving to be a difficult task. He and Eleanor wanted to live in the City, where Eleanor could keep her position as Charles' governess and he could continue his writing. The hamlet held no prospects for them at all and since Mr and Mrs Hyde had already gifted them with the opportunity to make use of the huge attic space as their first home together, August knew that it would cause nothing but problems if they were to live in the hamlet, with the only advantage being that they could easily afford to rent one of the cottages or even have the burnt-out shell of Prudence's old home rebuilt.

Having left Duke and the horse cart in the High street stables, August hurried through the city, anxious to be with his beloved Eleanor. It was becoming too painful being parted from her for most of the week and their wedding day couldn't come soon enough. He stopped by a street seller, barely visible behind his copious blooms of freshly cut flowers. Their sweet perfume caught in the light breeze as August impulsively asked the costermonger to put together a bouquet of multi-coloured lilies. Smoothing down his moustache as he arrived at the Hyde's residence, Eleanor swiftly pulled the door open wide and practically jumped into his arms before he could even reach the door knocker.

"Why, Miss Whitlock! That's no way for a young lady to conduct herself! What will the neighbours say!" teased August, overjoyed to hold Eleanor in his embrace at last.

"Oh, August! You will never, in a hundred years, believe what good news I have!"

August smiled widely as Eleanor took a backward step and ushered him into the vestibule.

"Oh! August! You bought me flowers!"

"Hmm, you've succeeded in detaching a few of the flowers from their stalks though!" he laughed as they viewed the scattering of petals at their feet.

"That's what the people do in India! They throw petals at the feet of the prince and princess...I think! But thank you, my darling, they smell divine!" With her nose immersed in the bouquet, Eleanor took a deep sniff before exploding into a bout of sneezes.

"What on earth are you two love birds doing out here?" declared Wilma Hyde, as she came out of the drawing-room. She looked down at the detached flower heads before issuing August and Eleanor with a most curious look. Felicity was resting happily on her hip with one hand holding onto Wilma's dark curls while the other arm jerked excitedly as she viewed August and Eleanor. At eight months old she had become the most popular and cherished member of the Hyde household, never failing to amuse everyone with her charming antics. Charles now adored her and protected her as a true older brother should, he was even teaching her to play the piano, though found it quite frustrating when Felicity simply preferred to smack the keys with her podgy hands and giggle.

"Have you told August yet?" quizzed Wilma.

"I wish somebody would tell me!" begged, August, "I can see that whatever it is, it has caused Ellie to be in the highest of spirits!" Wilma Hyde couldn't wait a second longer, "Mr Hyde has purchased the house next door! The deal will be signed and the house will be ours around the same time as you two dears marry!"

August still looked puzzled and not wanting to jump to any conclusions which might appear rude he waited for a further and more detailed explanation. Felicity had now released her hold on her mother's hair and was stretching her arms out to August.

"She does so adore you, August!"

"As I do her, Mrs Hyde," he affirmed, as he took her in his arms.

Eleanor tickled her tummy, "You are a little sweetheart, aren't you, Felicity!" A huge gummy smile made them all laugh out loud.

"Come along!" uttered Wilma, impatiently, "Let's take tea in the drawing-room and explain our wonderful plan to August!"

Austin and Wilma Hyde took it in turns to go over, what they considered to be, their brilliant plan which they'd anticipated would keep everyone happy.

The house next door was a duplicate of their own house and by chance, the elderly widower, whose family had all grown up and flown the nest many years ago had decided to take his son up on the invitation to live with him and his brood on his croft in the Scottish Highlands; tempted by the fact that a bountiful river flowed through the land, making it ideal for fishing, the gentleman was now finding living by himself a lonely struggle and since he seldom left his home anymore, his previous excuses that he'd miss Oxford too much now seemed irrelevant and he did, in fact, yearn for the company of his family.

Austin went on to explain how purchasing the house would be a sound investment for his family, but the main of his conversation was how the downstairs rooms, which consisted of three large reception rooms and a kitchen should be allocated to August's mother and Eleanor's grandmother. The upstairs rooms could be for Tilly, with one for Rosa when it was too late or when she was too tired to travel back to her parent's home. Since August and Eleanor were to live in the attic in the Hyde's home, which was already undergoing refurbishments,

Tilly and Eleanor's present room would make a larger playroom and nursery for Felicity. Wilma spoke of how she'd considered August and Eleanor occupying the upstairs of the new house, but was of the strong opinion that a newly married couple might find it rather *too* close for comfort and she believed newlyweds needed their privacy which the attic space would provide. She was insistent though, that should they wish, she was open to listening to all alternative suggestions to their ideas.

All eyes were suddenly focused on August since he was the only one who'd yet to hear the news. He churned the surprising news over in his head; delighted with what he'd heard, but knew that the most difficult part would be to convince his mother and even more so, to persuade Eleanor's grandmother to leave East Hanwell; they had both spent most of their lives there and had a treasure of memories attached to the sleepy hamlet.

"I don't think I can thank you enough, Mr Hyde...and Mrs Hyde, this is simply wonderful news, and far beyond anything I could ever have imagined!"

"Come now, August there's no need to turn so formal all of a sudden, we are one big and slightly unconventional family here and nobody knows better than Wilma and myself what it's like to begin married life with a struggle...isn't that correct, my darling?"

"Many years ago now, my dearest, but never a truer word spoken," confirmed Wilma Hyde. "I do so hope that your family in East Hanwell will come around to moving into the City, I'm sure they will grow to love it here and Charles and Felicity will rejoice in having *two* grandmothers living next door and of course, they can pop in here whenever they wish!"

"Oh yes!" cried Eleanor in jubilation, "I hadn't thought of that! They will have plenty to occupy themselves with here, it will make a change from the boring life they have at the moment and there'll be so much more space for them and then there's the beautiful garden which they can tend to…Oh August, we simply must persuade them!"

"Your quite right, Ellie, and we'll have peace of mind having them so close to us, especially during the winter months!"

Charles suddenly burst into the room, his arms laden with apples.

"Look! Felicity, I picked *all these* apples, just for you!"

Everyone was in awe of the sweet and considerate gift he presented to his sister, who was now sat playing happily with Tilly.

"I will stew a couple of them for her, Charles, she's still too young to eat apples straight from the tree!" stressed Tilly. "What a lovely brother you are!"

"They were straight from the ground, not the

tree! The wind has blown hundreds off...can you make an apple pie, Tilly?"

"Not today Master Charles, but I'm sure Rosa will make half a dozen tomorrow when she sees all the apples you've collected!"

With that Charles hurriedly announced that he was going to gather the rest of the windfalls before the birds and squirrels got to them.

"How will my mother and your grandmother be able to refuse the opportunity of spending time with such a polite and adorable young man?" questioned August, "Not to mention the adorable young, Miss Felicity!"

"I suggest you bring them here for a day, first, before the wedding...I'm sure Mr Wilson won't object to showing them around the house and they can get to know all of us, too! Perhaps it will help persuade them," suggested Wilma.

It seemed like an excellent idea, to which Eleanor and August both agreed to.

"Now, talking about the issue of persuading," continued Wilma, "have you managed to persuade Eleanor to invite her half-sister to the wedding, August?"

"Hmmm, I'm afraid not," confessed August.

"I don't want anything to ruin our special day, Mrs Hyde and I have an ominous feeling that she will prove bad news! Besides, she hasn't even had the decency to write to me since August's correspondence in which he informed her that he'd been united with me, at long last!"

"You should write again!" suggested Austin. "You know how sometimes mail can go astray, especially when it's going to such a hectic City as London!"

"Maybe I might be persuaded to seek her out after our wedding but until then, as I've lived my entire life without a half-sister, the only true sister at my wedding will be, dear Tilly."

# CHAPTER TWO

"Oh my Dear Lord!" hollered Peggy after she'd heard the loud thud and then witnessed Mr Levi's frail body at the foot of the stairs. She hurried down to him, as he whimpered quietly like a pitiful animal. His screwed up, pale face immediately informed her that he was in unbearable pain.

"How many times have I mentioned how that wobbly stair would cause an accident one day!" she cried out.

"Ah! What's done is done, Peggy! It is no use to cry over the milk which has been spilt, huh? Now help an old man to his bed...I will be fine!"

"Rayne! Rayne!" Peggy screamed at the top of her voice, becoming annoyed by her granddaughter's failure in hearing the commotion which was taking place."

Rayne was sat up in the attic which had become a storeroom since she and Peggy had left Castle Alley to move in with Uncle Levi. It was also a place where she could get away from the old folk, as she secretly referred to them, and have some peaceful, alone time. She had been reading the letter from August Miller once again. It never failed to bring her jealous blood to the boil, sparking wicked thoughts in her head. It had been the worst news she'd ever read in her life. August had been reunited with his precious

Eleanor and they were planning to marry. She had snatched the letter out of the postman's hands as she'd left the house on that morning back in April; hoping that it was a letter to say that he was planning a trip to Whitechapel, Rayne felt as though her world had been torn from beneath her as she read its brief and unpleasant contents. Even though the sun shone brightly and the birds seemed to be celebrating, on that spring morning, Rayne could not get her fiddle to play the light and joyful little tunes which the Whitechapel folk deserved to hear. August Miller was making a huge mistake and she knew that Eleanor Whitlock would ruin his life just as her mother had ruined her poor pappa's life! Those Whitlock women were conniving and wicked, she concluded and they seemed capable of hypnotism when it came to snaring a man. She had kept the letter a secret from her grandmother, knowing that she would be overjoyed by the news and perhaps insist on inviting both August and Eleanor to Whitechapel. Her reverie was suddenly broken as she heard her grandmother's distraught voice screaming her name.

"Coming, Grandmamma!"

Shocked by the sight of poor Uncle Levi appearing in so much pain and lying flat on his back in the hallway, Rayne practically flew down the stairs to be at his side.

"He tripped and fell down the stairs!" confirmed

Peggy, crossly. "Help me get him back upstairs to his room, Rayne."

Agonised from the slightest of movements, Mr Levi yelled out in distress.

"We can't possibly carry him upstairs, Grandmamma; we should let him rest in the parlour."

"Go and see if there's a palliasse up in the attic, Rayne while I fetch a blanket, the poor man is shivering! He's in shock!"

An hour later, Mr Levi was stretched out upon a palliasse on the parlour floor near the fireplace. With two thick blankets covering him and the fire burning, even though it was a mild September's day, Mr Levi continued to shiver. Peggy assisted him to drink a cup of hot sweet tea, while Rayne hurried to fetch the Doctor. There was little the Doctor could do for a man in his seventies with a suspected broken pelvis, apart from securing splints on his legs and leaving Peggy a large bottle of laudanum to administer to him. The prognosis wasn't good, the Doctor solemnly stated, it was unlikely that a man of Mr Levi's old age would last more than a week at the most and he left both Peggy and Rayne, trying desperately hard to conceal their watery eyes and their sadness from poor Mr Levi.

"I'm dying aren't I?" declared Mr Levi as soon as they returned to his side. "Don't try and hide it from me, I've been around on this fair earth for far too many years and seen men die before my eyes! I do not fear death; my aged bones are hollow and weak, I feel tired of life all of a sudden, and what better way to leave this world than with the two prettiest women of Whitechapel at my side!" It was clear that Mr Levi was putting on a brave face and heroically talking like an injured soldier on the battleground. "Rayne, my dear child, play your Uncle Levi a tune...the one you played me on that far off day when we first struck our business deal!"

With tears in her eyes, Rayne played a gentle lullaby which worked its magic and sent Mr Levi into a light sleep. As they cared for him around the clock, never leaving him on his own for longer than a few minutes, the worry of where they would go once Mr Levi had lost his fight for life played on both their minds, although nothing was ever spoken on the matter. The Doctor returned after a couple of days with more laudanum and although hiding his surprise, there was no fooling Peggy of his hidden shock to find Mr Levi still alive. He spoke quietly to Peggy, before leaving,

"I think he's hanging on for you and you must let him go! He's an old and a very sick man in a lot of pain; it would be kinder for you to leave him alone and let him slip away peacefully!"

As every muscle in her body became tense,

Peggy felt an overwhelming urge to issue the heartless doctor with a hard slap around his smug face and only just managed to keep her hands to herself, but her tongue was desperate to speak her mind,

"Would you wish to leave this world without your devoted family around your bed, when your time comes, Doctor? Mr Levi has no family and me and my granddaughter are going to make sure he wants for nothing in his final days. He has been good to us, has Mr Levi, and doesn't deserve to be left alone to die, as you so coldly put it! In fact, I've never in all my life heard such a load of old cod's wallop!"

"I will return in a couple of days if I'm not needed before! Good day to you, madam!" mumbled the doctor, unable to leave quick enough. Peggy was glad to see the back of him. Later that same evening, Mr Levi took a turn for the worse and was now burning up with a fever and drifting in and out of consciousness. Rayne and Peggy sat on either side of him, with Rayne playing an occasional peaceful tune, not even sure if he could hear it anymore as Peggy dosed him up with small sips of laudanum. He had spoken little but had insisted that when he left the world Peggy should take his savings which, he informed her, were hidden in the back of a broken carriage clock inside his wardrobe. He stressed how it wasn't a huge amount for a man of his age, but it would ensure that Peggy and

Rayne would be able to support themselves and perhaps Peggy could take out a lease on the grocery shop which she'd often talked about, but whatever they did it would at least keep them out of the workhouse. He told them how he had promised his entire stock to be donated to the Whitechapel orphanage, having grown up there, since his dear mother had passed away; it was his way of repaying them for his early years and would make for a quick clean-up of his worldly goods. News travelled fast on the streets and a stream of East End folk, most of whom had known Mr Levi all their lives, soon made their way through the pawnbroker's shop and into the parlour. As many wished him a speedy recovery, the majority sensed that it was their final goodbye to a man who had helped bail them out of financial difficulties on many occasions. Mr Levi had not been an overpowering pawnbroker but a fair and just one; he had always been ready to listen to reason and was a well-respected and loved man who everyone called Uncle Levi. He would be sadly missed and leave a huge void in Whitechapel. Word on the street of Mr Levi's impending death had also reached the infamous and much feared, Buster Forbes, who was waiting patiently to reclaim his property and finally make some money from the place. But his main interest in the death of his tenant was with the lodgers who had taken up residency with him. He considered it to be his lucky day when he'd run into Tommy Kettle not so long ago. Tommy was a good young man with a heart of gold but he was also weak and could be easily persuaded when it came to dropping a few 'missing' crates of merchandise his way. Always content with the lowest price which Buster was prepared to pay, he'd never once attempted to raise the price, not even when the merchandise was worth ten times the amount. He had caught Tommy one evening in the Salty Dog, a popular alehouse close by the river's edge frequented mostly by the thirsty dockers and sailors. Slouched in the corner, alone with his brass tankard, Buster immediately sensed something was wrong and made a beeline towards him. Tommy Kettle was a vital cog in his well-oiled underworld business dealings and was worth keeping a watchful eye on. An eerie but short-lived silence rippled through the alehouse the second that Buster Forbes's presence was noticed. He carried his bulky weight gracefully beneath his finely tailored, merino wool, twill suit which like all of his suits had been tailored in Saville Row. The aroma of sandalwood and Bergamot soon overpowered the stench of body odour and unwashed clothes, Buster made a point of applying his cologne quite liberally when frequenting the alehouses of the East End; he relished in being noticed and got a thrill out of putting fear into the common folk.

"Me dear old friend, Tommy Kettle!" he declared, bringing Tommy out of his dark thoughts. Buster pulled out his silver hip flask and proceeded to top up Tommy's tankard with the fine Scottish whiskey, one in fact which Tommy himself had unknowingly sold to him at a mere fraction of its street price.

"Wiv a face like that, it 'as ter be finances or females!" Buster dragged the wooden stool out from under the table, brushing it off with his fresh, white handkerchief before sitting down. Tommy tasted the spiked ale before greeting Buster, not caring if Buster considered him disrespectful on this occasion. Buster added some more whiskey to the tankard before taking a swig from the hip flask himself, licking his lips afterwards in appreciation of its quality. Tommy said nothing and continued to hang his head in misery.

"If it's funding yer short ov, lad, I'll be more than willing ter see yer right til' next shipment comes my way but when it comes ter affairs ov the heart, well, in me own experience, best thing ter do is ter keep busy an' spend a few shillings on a floozy!"

"D'yer ever know when a lass truly loves yer, Mister Forbes? I fought Rayne was gonna stick by me side fer ever... "

"Ah, son...there ain't no such thing as fer ever when it comes ter petticoats...they are a fickle species an' ain't never ter be trusted. Bin in love meself, more times than I can count on me fingers an' toes! Nah, women 'round 'ere just want a good time unless they get caught out an' find 'emselves in the family way...then they'll stick by yer, that's fer sure! Who is this Rayne lass then? Can't say I've ever 'eard of a cove 'round 'ere naming 'is bint, Rayne!"

"Folk know her more as, *the fiddle girl!*"

*"Now it makes sense!"* expressed Buster, quickly taking another mouthful from his hip flask. "I've seen that pretty young maiden an' 'eard the sweet music she plays, an' all. Never in all me days would 'ave believed she'd be interested in the likes of a lanky docker though! She looks a bit too classy; I bet she don't even live in the East End!" Buster smoothed his horseshoe moustache, waiting for Tommy's reaction; he felt he might have been a little harsh with his wording on the obviously heartbroken, young man.

"She lives above Levi's pawnbroker's with 'er grandmother, but she is new ter these parts, an' up until 'er father passed away she was a stranger ter the East End!"

"I'm intrigued, *Mr Kettle*, please tell me more."

# CHAPTER THREE

An ominous gale had blown in from the North East bringing blustery showers with it and as Peggy viewed the change in weather as being the end to the summer of 1878, she also considered it to be an ill omen and sensed that in such stormy weather, her dear friend's soul would soon be taken away to the heavens. Her dark premonition proved true and as the candles flickered in the shadowy parlour, Mr Levi breathed his last breath and as Peggy kissed him for the first and last time and placed the copper pennies on his eyelids, Rayne burst into tumultuous sobs.

"Mr Levi was the salt of the earth, but he's out of his terrible pain now and gone to a far better place, Rayne, so we should give thanks that the Good Lord took mercy on him and released him from his suffering. He made old bones and was loved by many folk and I, for one, consider myself blessed to have known him and shared a little portion of my life with him." As a stream of tears gently trickled down Peggy's cheek, in the back of her mind the reality that she and Rayne would soon find themselves homeless in Whitechapel, couldn't be ignored. Rayne's dramatic display of grief soon came to an abrupt end as she too remembered that it was Uncle Levi's home they were living in; she'd become so used to her new home and had often forgotten how it was only through the kind-heartedness of dear old Uncle Levi that they'd been able to vacate the awful squalor of their lodgings in Castle Alley, so quickly.

"As soon as you set eyes on Tommy, make sure to ask him to look out for some decent lodgings for us, Rayne; he knows everything and everybody this side of the river!"

"I will Grandmamma, don't you worry now, I'm sure we will be fine and don't forget, we have Uncle Levi's savings which he bequeathed to you!"

"Rayne! How could you mention that with poor Mr Levi not even in his place of rest yet and barely cold!" scolded Peggy.

Rayne let out a long sigh as she remembered the awkward experience she'd had to undergo the last time that she was with Tommy Kettle and of which she had not yet mentioned to her grandmother. Tommy had been stood watching her play for longer than usual on that stifling August day. She had glanced at him more than half a dozen times and noticed how distracted he appeared. She had wondered why he'd arrived to escort her home so early and why he was wearing his Sunday best. Cutting her performance short, in fear that perhaps Tommy had heard some bad news, Rayne quickly concealed the violin from her complaining audience who were begging her to continue, declaring that it had a broken string. She hastened to Tommy's side still aware of his nervous stance.

"Hello, Tommy, what brings you here so early today?"

"I needed to talk to yer, Rayne." Although smiling widely, Tommy still appeared awkward and on edge. He fiddled with his hands before stuffing them deep into his pockets.

"I stopped playing early, Tommy. I thought you looked perturbed standing in the crowd...*what is it?*"

"Let's go an 'ave some Rosie lee, Rayne, me throat is as dry as a sheet ov sandpaper! We'll go ter one of them fancy tea rooms that yer like!"

"Goodness Tommy, you already look awkward enough standing in the street; I don't think I could risk the embarrassment of accompanying you into a tea room and witness you holding delicate teacups!" giggled Rayne.

" So d'yer reckon I ain't good enough ter drink tea in one of them places then, is that what yer mean, Rayne! I can be as fancy as that August Miller cove if I wants ter be, yer know!"

"What's August Miller got to do with it...have you seen him by chance? Is he here in Whitechapel?" inquired Rayne, excitedly.

Tommy became quiet, and as Rayne viewed his angry expression, she suddenly realised what was eating Tommy and why he'd arrived so early at Covent Garden; August *was* in Whitechapel and Tommy didn't want them to bump into each other. If she didn't know better, she could swear that Tommy was green with jealousy.

"*No!*" he snapped belligerently. "Yer precious bleedin' Miller ain't in Whitechapel, an' if 'e is, I ain't caught sight ov 'im!"

"Ooh, somebody's a bit green I believe!" teased Rayne, now wishing she'd ignored Tommy in the crowd and continued playing her music.

"You'd be wiser ter forget that cove, Rayne, 'e's in love with another an' yer don't stand a chance if you've got ideas on 'im!"

"I can't possibly forget the handsome August Miller, my *dear Tommy* because if you remember, when he finds his precious little Eleanor, he will also be finding my half-sister, which gives me the perfect excuse to show my face and persuade him that I am, by far, a better catch and more suited to him then that illegitimate brat will ever be! At least I have good breeding and I'm artistically talented, just as he is! We would make a perfect couple I believe!"

Tommy suddenly grabbed both her arms and twirled her body around to face him, "Yer talkin' nonsense, Rayne, an' yer knows it! Marry me...I'll make yer 'appy an' proud! I'm not always gonna be a docker yer know...One day I plan ter 'ave me own business! We make a perfect couple...*look!*" Quickly releasing her arms he pulled out a small box from his inside, jacket pocket. Rayne felt quite nauseous all of a sudden, knowing what was inside it. He sprung it open, and surprisingly a most beautiful gold ring with a huge rectangular emerald surrounded by petite diamonds, dazzled beneath the glaring sun.

Lost for words, Rayne could only gaze down at the ring in disbelief; she would never have credited Tommy Kettle to purchase such an exquisite and attractive ring. He removed it from its small velvet cushion and took Rayne's hand.

"Try it on, darlin', it might need ter be adjusted."

She stood in a daze as he slipped the ring onto the third finger of her left hand. It was a perfect fit, as though it had been specially made for her slender finger. She loved the ring, it sparkled and suited her hand, but she didn't love Tommy Kettle and certainly didn't want to spend the rest of her life with him.

"We could be married in the spring, or sooner if yer don't wanna wait that long!"

Tommy's words began to dance around inside her head. What was she doing, she suddenly thought as she hurriedly yanked the ring from her finger as though it was burning her flesh.

"It's truly a lovely ring, Tommy, but I could never marry you...you're my friend and that is as far as our relationship will ever stretch to!"

"But I love yer, Rayne! I ain't never loved no other lass in me life like I love you...please marry me, Rayne...I know I can make yer 'appy. Please, Rayne!"

As he stood in the street yelling out his feelings, Rayne was engulfed with a spontaneous instinct that she didn't even want to remain his friend anymore; she wanted nothing at all to do with Tommy Kettle from this day forth.

"Leave me alone Tommy, I never wish to see you again! *Do you understand?*"

Rayne quickly turned and ran as fast as she could, disappearing into the crowds and hopefully seeing the last of Tommy.

From the day when Mr Levi had been laid to rest in the Whitechapel cemetery, everything seemed to move at lightning speed. Peggy and Rayne had already begun boxing up the stock ready to be delivered to the orphanage, but also in the hope that they might come across Mr Levi's broken carriage clock which was not to be found in his wardrobe, where he'd instructed it to be or anywhere else in the house. Peggy was convinced that in his old age, Mr Levi's sometimes confused mind had forgotten where he'd placed it for safekeeping.

With the recent disaster on the third of September, when the pleasure steamer, *'The princess Alice'* had been hit by a collier ship on the River Thames as it returned from Sheerness, much of Whitechapel was already in mourning. It was estimated that more than six hundred men, women and children had lost their lives on that fated day, including many locals and a dozen or so customers who often frequented the grocery where Peggy worked. The sombre atmosphere and the bleak outlook seemed to affect Rayne far more than Peggy. She'd witnessed enough misery and found that the only way to escape her depression was to constantly daydream about August Miller, and try to devise ways in which she could find a way into his life and hopefully into his heart.

They were also called on by a couple of aloof and threatening men, who it transpired, were employed by the infamous Buster Forbes whose seedy underworld empire claimed ownership to the pawnbroker's shop and the dwelling above it. They vulgarly insisted that the premises were to be vacated by the end of the week; even though Mr Levi's lease didn't end for another five months, but since they were not family, Peggy and Rayne had no legal rights to remain and as the men had informed them, they were being exceedingly generous in even allowing them to remain for a few extra days when it was within their rights to turn them out onto the street immediately. In a sudden state of panic, both Peggy and Rayne had little sleep from that day forth, while they spent every hour turning the house upside down, frantically hunting high and low for the elusive carriage clock.

"I have an awful feeling that Mr Levi threw that

broken old clock out with the rest of his useless stock during that sort out we had when we were snowed under, back in January!" concluded Peggy when there was nowhere else left to look.

"Don't worry Grandmamma, something will turn up, you and I are usually quite lucky and I will just have to try and find work in a music hall and you have your job in the grocery. We'll be fine and we have lots of friends in Whitechapel now!"

"We do indeed, but most of them are poorer than us and live ten to a room! We have been living in luxury here! The future doesn't bode well, my darling!"

# CHAPTER FOUR

It had been well worth emptying his finest malt whiskey down Tommy Kettle's throat, mused Buster Forbes as he leaned back in his leather upholstered chair with his shining black boots resting on his desk. He drew in a deep lung full of cigar smoke as a multitude of thoughts ticked over in his head. What an uncanny coincidence that the sweet and innocent young fiddle girl of Whitechapel should turn out to be none other than Edward Jackson's daughter, he mused. After the inconvenient and sudden death of Jackson, Buster had felt totally deflated knowing that his plans on getting even with the unscrupulous crook had also died but even though Jackson was cold in his grave, nothing would satisfy Buster more than to mark a cruel stain on Jackson's progeny and get even. He had been in his early twenties when Edward Jackson had employed him to do his dirty work, sending him off in the dark hours of the night to meet up with the most ruthless villains of the East End. Buster had put his life at stake more times than he cared to remember and his body carried the multiple scars as a reminder of how close he'd come to meeting his Maker. He ran his fingers over the deep crevice which stretched from below his ear lobe to his collar bone and shuddered as nauseating memories flooded his thoughts of how he'd been left to bleed to death after a deal to buy a stolen haul of solid silver pocket watches had gone wrong. The band of notorious thieves were one step ahead of Buster; he had been naive and too trusting of that great man, Jackson, who until that moment he'd admired and aspired to be like one day. While Jackson sat by the warmth of his blazing office fire, anticipating how wealthy the hoard was about to make him, the unforgiving gang immediately spotted that the crisp white banknotes were fake. They were far from amused and didn't pause for thought before laying into Buster with their angry fists and heavy boots before slashing his neck, declaring how Buster would think twice in the future before attempting to con any of their East End associates; it was their code of practice and the honour amongst thieves which was not to be taken lightly. Buster had lain in a pool of blood, unconscious and near to bleeding to death before being rescued and taken to the London Hospital where he fought for his life for three long weeks. Edward Jackson, meanwhile, suddenly vanished and had left no word with anyone of where he'd gone or when or if he would ever return. But return he did, some ten months later and instead of seeking him out and attempting to make amends; Jackson ignored him as though he'd never even known of any young man called Buster Forbes.

Sickened by Edward Jackson's cowardly

behaviour, it was a turning point for Buster and from that day forth he went about establishing his own wheeling and dealing business, vowing to treat any workers he might employ in the future with kindness and also vowing to get even with Jackson, one day.

But with his vows failing, at thirty-five, Buster had transformed into a notorious and much-feared gang leader with an unhealthy monopoly on copious local dwellings and businesses. Toughened by a life from the cradle of poverty and hardship, the men of the East End only seemed to understand one kind of language and that was brute force. Buster prided himself, though, that as yet, he'd never put an end to anyone's life.

Now, as he sat mulling over how he was going to proceed with turning Edward Jackson in his grave the familiar sound of Big Ben in the distance chimed four times, but Buster's mind was too alert and sleep could wait. Since he already had a trump card to play, being the owner of the pawnbroker's which old Levi had occupied for so long, a sly smirk covered Buster's worn face as he decided to call on the property at first light.

"Grandmamma! Come quickly, there's a man down in the shop! He wants to have a word with you!"

Rayne was flustered; the stranger had caught her

off guard as she'd been sat in the shop, treating her violin to a coat of beeswax. Buster Forbes had stood silently admiring Edward Jackson's daughter for a few minutes before planting his foot down heavily to gain her attention. Taken by complete surprise and alarmed by the authoritative charisma of the well-groomed, stranger, Rayne just managed to catch his words as he asked to see her Grandmother. Whoever he was, she mused, he obviously knew who she and her grandmother were.

With her head held high and her chest puffed out like a dominant mother hen, Peggy hurried into the shop, presuming it was just another trickster making out that Mr Levi owed him money. Buster had already taken the liberty of making his way to the other side of the shop's counter, startling Peggy, and causing her to scream out in alarm. After a quick inspection of the heavily built man, who seemed to fill the entire shop with his presence, Peggy sensed by his stylish and expensive attire, that he was of a higher ranking than a common crook out to cadge a couple of shillings.

He doffed his top hat and greeted Peggy with a broad smile, displaying slightly yellowed teeth.

"I do apologise if I caused yer any alarm by my presence, Mrs...I'm sorry, but are you also a Jackson like yer granddaughter?"

Finding it difficult to suppress her anger, Peggy took in a deep breath, as she tried to compose herself.

"I'm not a Jackson, I'm Peggy Bow! Mrs Peggy Bow, though why it's any of your business, I fail to see! Now, say what you came here to say and kindly vacate my home!"

Buster couldn't help but laugh, infuriating Peggy even more. He took a step closer to her, removed his top hat, and calmly placed it on the counter.

"I think you'll find, Mrs Bow, that me humble hat 'as more legal rights in this 'ere building than you or yer granddaughter do. Allow me ter introduce meself, I am Buster Forbes and this is my property!"

Lost for words, Peggy merely stood in silence, but her thoughts were churning over like a steam engine. Buster Forbes, she mused, it was a name she'd heard before and not through Mr Levi, but where and when she couldn't quite recall.

"So, the late Edward Jackson was, in fact, yer son in law, then?" he continued, breaking into Peggy's reverie.

"I don't see what that has to do with anything, but yes, he was, and my granddaughter and me will be leaving your property by the end of the week, just as we were told by, who I'm presuming, were your henchmen!"

Throwing his head back and laughing emphatically, Buster was enjoying every minute in the company of Peggy as she took a cautious stance.

"My dear, Mrs Bow, I've arrived 'ere ter offer yer assistance, not ter hurl yer out on ter the streets! Do I look the sort ter intimidate defenceless women? I've got a proposition ter put before yer sweet ears!"

Rayne, who had been listening in on the conversation behind the half-opened door, decided it was time she made an entrance. Buster was immediately distracted as he feasted his eyes on the pretty young maiden; he could quite see why Tommy Kettle had been so distraught by her refusal to marry him, but at the same instant knew she could do far better than commit herself to an ignorant docker, like Tommy.

"Ah, the talented young 'fiddle girl!'"

"This is Mr Forbes, Rayne," stated Peggy, abruptly. "He owns Mr Levi's shop! *Apparently!*"

"Oh yes, poor Mr Levi, he was the salt of Whitechapel, a man just like myself, wiv a heart ov gold!"

"Yes, Mr Levi was indeed a kind and decent sort," agreed Peggy.

"Play me a tune, Miss Jackson!" Buster suddenly demanded.

Taken by surprise by his out of the blue request, Rayne glanced to her grandmother, who was wearing an extremely cross face.

"Just because you own this roof, doesn't mean you can march in here and order me or my granddaughter about, Mr Forbes!"

In a finely tuned voice, Buster shifted all of his attention towards Rayne, "Would you care to play me a tune, Miss Jackson. *Please!*"

Buster was suddenly laughing uncontrollably as he viewed Rayne take out her handkerchief and lay it upon the shop's counter before she picked up her instrument.

"I admire yer way ov thinking, *fiddle girl!* Reckon you'll make yer fortune one day!"

Beginning with her chirpy street tunes, as she viewed Buster depositing a few coins onto the handkerchief every couple of minutes, she then proceeded to play some of Mr Levi's favourite and much longer compositions by the famous violinist, Pierre Baillot.

"Beautiful! Beautiful!" Buster cried out after fifteen minutes had passed and he'd emptied his entire pocket full of change onto Rayne's handkerchief.

"That's what I call a good morning's work!" declared Rayne, scooping up the pile of coins, "And I didn't even have to walk all the way to Covent Garden!"

Buster chuckled, he liked Rayne, even though she was Edward Jackson's daughter and he now felt confident that she'd prove a valuable asset in increasing his already healthy bank balance.

"I'm planning on opening a music hall in Whitechapel!" he announced. "Work for me, Miss Jackson, you will be top of the bill! What d'yer reckon, Mrs Bow?"

Peggy was uncertain, sensing she had to be vigilant. There was something not quite right and she didn't trust Buster Forbes. Before she had a chance to reply, the shrewd East Ender added a little more temptation to his offer. "You could both carry on living 'ere, an' pay me rent, all proper ov course, an' you, Mrs Bow could run the pawnbroker's shop, or yer could change it ter whatever shop yer fancy?"

"Grandmamma!" cried Rayne, "you could open that grocery that you've been dreaming of!" Buster's smile suddenly widened, "Sounds like we'll all be 'appy!"

"Thank you, Mr Forbes, you're offer is very generous, but we need to think about it first before rushing into anything we might regret later!"

As Buster slowly replaced his top hat, Peggy got a glimpse of the unsightly scar on his neck. She felt her blood run cold as she suddenly remembered who Buster was and how Edward Jackson had been responsible for him coming so close to death when he'd been a younger man.

# CHAPTER FIVE

"I can't remember the last time I felt so happy in my life, Winifred!" expressed Prudence, with tears of joy in her eyes.

"Me too! And to think that I always envisioned taking my last breath in East Hanwell. I feel as though I'm about to go on a whole new adventure; it's like starting a new life!"

"Well, you are! And it is a huge new adventure! It certainly outweighs moping around here in this sleepy hamlet like a couple of old hens, just waiting for God! When I remember how I was all for giving up on life when I refused to leave my burning cottage, it makes me shudder! God bless, August for rescuing me as he did; many a young man wouldn't have been so insistent on saving a stubborn old woman like me! Not only did he save my life, but he found my darling little Eleanor! Never thought I would see her in this life, you know!"

"I know, Prudence! Think you must have told me that a hundred times or more! Now, are we going to pack what few belongings we possess or just sit reminiscing all morning! August said that he'd be here to collect us at midday and with the wedding tomorrow, I doubt he'll be in the mood to dilly dally!"

"I'm so overjoyed that they've decided to wed nearby in our local chapel, Winifred?"

Winifred gazed around the small room of the cottage which had been her home for a quarter of a century.

"I suppose in my heart of hearts I would have prefered it if they'd chosen to live here in East Hanwell, just as we did, but Ellie is not a hamlet girl, and I know how much August loves the City life too. They're a new generation, who expect more from life than we did when we were young, Prudence. Who knows, we might find that we come to love the City ways too!"

"Not me, I *love* that house in Paradise Street and I love the fact that I'm going to be part of my granddaughter's life, but I'm not sure how I feel about stepping outside and taking a stroll around Oxford! I'll more than likely get lost and never find my way home again!"

Winifred laughed, she was glad that at least she'd had more experience than Prudence and was not a stranger to Oxford's bustling City.

"Don't be so daft, Prudence, we will stroll together; I know my way around...used to sell bloomers down at the Wednesday market, you know, when August was just a boy!"

"Talking of boys, don't you just adore Mr and Mrs Hyde's young son, not to mention their beautiful baby daughter!"

"Oh, Prudence, it feels as though the Good Lord has blessed us with a brand new family...just what we need to keep us young at heart!"

"Let's finish the rest of that tea in the pot,

Winifred afore we pack, seems a shame to waste it!"

"You sit and finish the tea while I pack our belongings into that trunk which August gave us, besides most of your bits and bobs were lost in the fire and I don't have much; doubt it will take me more than half an hour!"

"Don't put our new dresses in that trunk, Winifred, we don't want them looking as though we've been sleeping in them, come tomorrow!"

It was an hour before midday when Prudence and Winifred heard the familiar sound of the carriage wheels upon the dirt track, adjacent to the hamlet. August had hired a carriage for the journey; since old Duke belonged to the hamlet folk and was needed during harvest time. Purposely arriving earlier than arranged, August didn't want his ma or Prudence to be sat in sorrow as they dwelt on all their memories which East Hanwell harboured. He and Eleanor were still quite shocked at how easy it had been to persuade them to make the move and didn't want to risk anything changing their minds again.

As was expected, they were ready and waiting and looking like a couple of lost souls about to be lead off to foreign parts. They were sat outside enjoying the pleasant but weak, October sun; upon the wooden bench which August had made for his ma when he was fourteen; two tree stumps with a plank of wood nailed to them. He had been so proud when he'd presented it to her and she had since spent many hours making good use of it.

"Don't you two, handsome ladies look just like a fine oil painting!" he declared, as he jumped out of the carriage.

Lost for words, Prudence and Winifred were stunned by the fancy carriage and were paying more attention to the driver as he carried the trunk, as though it were nothing more than a loaf of bread, hoisting it effortlessly onto the back of the carriage.

"You need to look after your money, August!" declared Winifred. "That must have cost a man's monthly wage to hire out!"

"It's a special occasion, Ma! Today is the beginning of a new way of life for *all* of us! It deserves to be remembered with style! Now come along, Rosa and Tilly are preparing a grand welcoming meal for you, and Charles hasn't stopped asking when you will be arriving all week long!"

Winifred took one last look at the cottage, while Prudence stared deep in thought at the spot where her home had once stood. August kept silent allowing them to fill up their hearts and minds with treasured memories.

"You'll never guess who's moving into our old cottage, son!" declared Winifred, as she quickly wiped away a falling tear. "Iris Fielding finally accepted Robin Hardy's marriage proposal; she's taken second best, you know? That poor girl always lived in hope that, one day, you would notice her, August!"

August sighed beneath his breath; his mother's news was music to his ears, but he couldn't understand why she was trying to make him feel guilty.

"I hope she loves, him," uttered Prudence, "because there's nothing worse than an empty union; it's a recipe for a miserable life!"

"Oh, Prudence! I wish I was a young lass again! Love is so beautiful, and produces beautiful babies!"

"Winifred! Act your age, you're embarrassing poor August, he's turned as red as a cherry!"

August assisted them into the carriage, as they giggled together, more like a pair of school girls than women in their later years.

The rest of the day passed by all too quickly as the Hyde's beautiful home became alive with the pre-wedding excitement and the arrival of August's mother and Eleanor's grandmother. The dining table was full, apart from Eleanor's place, as she was not permitted to see August on the day before their wedding. Rosa had taken her up a tray to the new and delightfully refurbished attic space. She was far too nervous though, and only a few mouthfuls of the delicious meal passed her lips. Winifred and

Prudence, felt as though Christmas had arrived two months early, they devoured the exquisite banquet set before them and relished in having so many new and friendly faces to converse with. Charles, as usual, kept everyone entertained by his amusing antics and anecdotes and when young Felicity put in an appearance after her midday nap, as usual, she melted everyone's hearts with her cuteness. The main topic of conversation was, of course, the impending wedding and with Wilma in her element, acting as the chief organiser, as soon as the meal had been eaten, Austin, August and Charles escaped to the garden for a little peace, leaving the womenfolk to go over every detail for the hundredth time and also allowing Eleanor to come out of hiding to join the high spirited party. All the women had contributed to the making of Eleanor's spectacular wedding gown, with Wilma cutting and sewing it, with the help of one of Hyde&Son's machines, and the other women painstakingly sewing hundreds of seed pearls to the bodice and train and adding the final, locally-made, lace.

"You must try your dress on, Eleanor...just one last time before tomorrow!" insisted Wilma, the second that she came downstairs.

Eleanor hurried to greet her grandmother, still finding it hard to believe that she was now part of her life and about to move in next door.

"Welcome to Paradise Street, Grandmamma,

and Mrs Miller, I can't even begin to tell you how happy you've made me...and August, of course."

Winifred had been wearing a continuous smile since the moment she'd arrived and even after the few months in which she'd known Eleanor she never ceased to be in awe of her beauty, convinced that she was becoming more attractive with every passing day.

"We can't have you calling me, Mrs Miller for the rest of my days, Eleanor!" expressed Winifred, as she greeted her, soon to be, daughter in law with a warm embrace. Feeling shy, all of a sudden, Eleanor felt her face glowing.

"What would you prefer me to call you, Mrs Miller?" she asked, in a small voice.

"You could call me, Ma, or Aunty? Whichever you prefer."

"Excuse me!" objected Prudence, overhearing Winifred's words. "Are you young enough to my daughter, Winifred? She can't be calling you Ma and me Grandmamma if the sums don't add up!"

"Goodness, Prudence, we are hardly likely to publish the news in the Oxford Journal! It's just within our surrounding walls, you know. Besides, I might just be young enough to be your daughter!"

Wilma, Tilly, Rosa, and Eleanor, all sat entertained by the amusing banter between the two elder women.

"You never did tell me how old you actually are, Prudence, but I've always presumed that you must be a good score of years my senior....your beautiful granddaughter is eighteen, after all!"

"Oh, very well, Winifred, I suppose I am old enough to be your mother, but only if I'd have born you when I was very young and don't go forgetting that! I'm about to start a new chapter in my life, you know!"

Remembering how Prudence had once wished for her life to end when her cottage had caught fire, Winifred felt her heart contract. Prudence had become a new woman since the discovery of Eleanor; she had a renewed vigour and even looked years younger than before. Winifred blinked away her tears as she took hold of Prudence's hand in hers, giving it a gentle squeeze.

"Tell you what, Prudence, Eleanor can call me Aunty, because you are more like my dear sister than my mother!"

The women gave a round of applause, causing both Winifred and Prudence to turn a shade of pink; they had, for the briefest of moments, forgotten that they were not in the privacy of Winifred's cottage in East Hanwell.

"Now! Tilly, you stand guard of the door, while Eleanor tries on her gown!" ordered Wilma, who was already removing the dress from its box.

"August Miller is about to marry the most

beautiful girl in Oxfordshire and no mistaking!"
declared Prudence.

"She hasn't even put the dress on yet!" said
Winifred.

"Ah! She doesn't need no fancy, gown, Winifred,
she'd look stunning in a coal sack!"

The tight-fitting bodice and the full, slightly
bustled skirt of cream silk gauze only
emphasized Eleanor's perfect figure and the
puffed lace, three quarter length sleeves with
their decorative silk bows added to the beauty of
the wedding ensemble. The garland of pale pink
and lemon rose buds with interwoven green
foliage fitted around Eleanor's head and was
attached to the elaborate train which cascaded
down her back in pretty ripples.

There was complete silence in the drawing-room
as Eleanor took centre stage, looking like a
stunning angel, and seaming to hypnotize the
women.

"It's a perfect fit, and I adore it! Thank you all so
much!" she declared, breaking the silence.

With compliments and praise flowing from
everyone lips, Eleanor wished she could just
walk up the aisle immediately and become
August's wife; another twenty hours seemed too
long for her to bear.

# CHAPTER SIX

It was the one request that Eleanor couldn't deny Mrs Miller and her grandmother, for her and August to marry in the small chapel just on the outskirts of East Hanwell and the neighbouring village of Lower Sompting. It had been the chapel in which both women had made their own wedding vows, many years before. Not marrying in St. Mary and St. John church would also mean that the day wouldn't constantly remind Eleanor that her poor mother was just outside the church doors, in the cemetery.

The day was blessed with unusually warm and sunny weather for the end of October; it was repeated by everyone as to how it was a wedding gift from the Almighty Himself for the deserving young couple. Eleanor and August wouldn't have minded a snow blizzard on their special day, they were both so elated that after the few years of torment each had suffered, they were about to be united as husband and wife and begin their much dreamt of life together.

The folk of East Hanwell and Lower Sompting had never witnessed such a grand parade of prestigious carriages arriving in their tranquil part of the world. Their local weddings were usually arrived at by foot.

Mr and Mrs Hyde had hired three of the finest carriages, one for themselves, Charles and

Felicity and of course Eleanor, who was to walk up the aisle on the arm of Austin Hyde. There was a carriage for Mrs Miller, Prudence and August and then another for Tilly, Rosa and Rosa's parents, who although had yet to meet Eleanor or August, had heard the continuous reports of their love story from Rosa and wished for nothing more than to be part of the wedding ceremony. The Reverend Doyle and his wife occupied another lavish-looking carriage and Doctor Thompson and his wife had decorated their small gig with the last of their garden's beautiful white and red roses. A procession of five gleaming carriages and nine handsome stallions trotted noisily through the Oxfordshire dirt tracks, alerting all of the residents who were ready and waiting to wave and cheer the procession on its way.

Wilma Hyde suddenly removed her lace glove, furtively licked her fingertips, as she attempted to organise Charles' out of control curls.

"We should have insisted that Rosa took him to the barber, Austin, his curls have a mind of their own!"

Charles tried to assist his ma, "I like my curls, Mamma and so does Miss Ellie...I don't want them cut off!"

"And where's your hat, Charles? Why isn't it on your head keeping your hair in place?"

"Because it refuses to stay on his head, my dear," voiced Austin, casually.

"I don't believe it! Austin! How could you be so lax, we are the owners of a reputable men's clothing store in the heart of Oxford! We have our reputation to consider!"

"Oh, Wilma, we are going to a tiny hamlet, miles out of the City, I doubt these folk have even heard of Hyde&Son, and they certainly wouldn't be able to afford our prices, as reasonable as they are!"

The dispute came to a sudden end as Felicity decided that she wanted to get down and crawl around on the grubby carriage floor, which of course was completely out of the question. Eleanor tried to amuse the infant and pondered on how upset Mrs Miller and Prudence would be if they'd have heard Mr Hyde's remarks. If there was one lesson which she'd learnt from visiting East Hanwell during the recent months, it was how proud the hamlet folk were and how they considered the City folk to be rather cold-hearted and aloof. She hoped that with Mrs Miller and Prudence now living next door to them such misunderstandings would soon be put right.

"Will I have to call you, Mrs Miller after today, Miss Ellie?" asked Charles.

"Of course you will, Charles!" expressed Wilma, abruptly, as she continued to flatten the lad's curls.

"I wouldn't mind if you continued to call me Mrs Ellie, if that's alright with your mamma, of course," stated Eleanor.

Just as they arrived outside of the tiny chapel, Felicity gave up her angry protest and fell asleep, prompting Austin to chuckle at his daughter's antics.

"Well, at least we might have a peaceful wedding, now!" voiced Wilma, with a sigh of relief. "I wonder if Mrs Miller would mind holding her in the chapel since Rosa and Tilly are to walk up the aisle behind Eleanor and I *must* be free to keep matters organised."

"*And me*, I'm walking too...I'm the page boy, remember!"

"Of course we remember, Charles!" stressed Wilma. "A page boy *without a hat!*"

"But his curls are far more fetching than a top hat, which might topple off his head  constantly, wouldn't you agree?" said Eleanor, suddenly feeling nervous as the coach driver opened the door and pulled down the steps

"Austin, Charles and Eleanor! You three remain in the coach until everyone is inside the chapel, we don't want August to see you, Eleanor and be careful with your gown, these coach doorways are exceedingly narrow," cautioned Wilma, as, once again, she admired the beautiful wedding dress.

"Oh, please allow me to hold the train, too, Miss Ellie!" begged Charles.

"Charles! If you don't behave yourself, I will shut you in this carriage and you will miss the wedding! It is not the duty of a page boy to hold the bride's train, now I don't want to hear another word pass your lips, is that understood?"

Charles nodded his head, solemnly as his mother let out an exaggerated sigh and Austin found it difficult not to smile as he looked on proudly at his son.

Carrying Felicity in her arms, Wilma made her way with the rest of the guests into the chapel while Tilly and Rosa joined Eleanor by her carriage.

"Oh, Ellie! I can hardly believe this day is happening! I'm sure I'm as excited as you!" cried Tilly. "You look so beautiful, Ellie; without doubt the most beautiful bride I've ever seen!"

"She's absolutely right, Ellie and taken the words from my mouth!" echoed Rosa. "I just know that you and August are going to be the happiest couple; you were made for each other!"

Eleanor felt as though her heart would explode, she wanted to remember every second of this special day and keep it safe in her heart forever.

"Oh, just look at you two! Your dresses are sublime! You are going to look like elegant swans gliding behind me! And I pray that one day it will be me attending your weddings!"

"Can we go now, Miss Ellie! Pappa, is it time for us to go inside the church now? *Please say yes!*" pestered Charles, becoming impatient and fed up with the women's chatter. Austin issued him with a warning glare.

The elderly vicar, who was to marry them, suddenly appeared outside of the chapel.

"Are you ready Eleanor, I think that's our cue to enter the chapel!"

Eleanor smiled nervously at Austin, whilst Tilly and Rosa took hold of her train and steered Charles into position.

The wedding breakfast was held in the Claredon Hotel in Cornmarket, just around the corner from Hyde&Son, Austin was well acquainted with the proprietor and had struck a reasonable deal with him with the addition of a free, Hyde& Son, suit into the bargain. Hotels, City life, and being surrounded by kind and friendly folk was like stepping into a new world for Winifred and Prudence. For too many years they had led a sheltered and mundane existence in the sleepy hamlet of East Hanwell and now as they sat in the pristine hotel dining room, relishing in the exquisite culinary delights, they were both overjoyed and euphoric about their change of circumstances.

Charles eyed the mountains of delicious-looking food, as he licked his lips, secretly hoping that he'd not be full until he'd tasted everything in sight. Wilma and Austin had struck up an instant friendship with Doctor Thompson and his wife and Tilly took the opportunity to chat to Reverend Doyle and his wife. Permanent smiles were etched upon the faces of Eleanor and

August, as they sat side by side, both feeling as though they were in a dream. Furtively taking her hand in his beneath the crisp white table cloth, August softly whispered, "I love you, Mrs Miller."

"Oh, August, am I really Mrs Miller! I never thought this day would come. I'm so happy, August!"

"When can we go home, my darling wife? I just want to kiss you and hold you. I want your sweet voice to be the only one I hear!"

A sudden flood of goosebumps rushed through Eleanor's entire body, she ached to be in August's arms and feel his lips kissing hers. She also felt nervous, as she remembered the motherly talk which Wilma had surprised her with a couple of evenings ago.

"We can't leave our own wedding, August, what would our guests think!" giggled Eleanor, timidly.

"Don't be nervous, my darling, you have nothing to fear from me, I intend to take you to heaven and back!"

"*August!* I can feel my cheeks glowing!"

"You look beautiful, my love; my radiant wife, my blushing bride!"

Austin and Wilma Hyde made their way towards them, both beaming.

"How are the two love birds then?"

"Austin! Don't embarrass them, remember how we felt on our wedding day!" ordered Wilma.

"Ah! Yes, how could I ever forget, my sweet turtle dove!"

He pulled out a key from his waistcoat pocket and handed it to August.

"We will see you in two days; you're booked into the bridal suite. Enjoy the peace and quiet of your brief honeymoon, Mr and Mrs Miller!"

It was an unexpected but much-appreciated surprise.

"I don't think Charles would give you any peace and Felicity is fast becoming an, out of tune, soprano singer. You two deserve a blissful start to your married life, even if it is only a couple of days!" added Wilma.

# CHAPTER SEVEN

November arrived with its notorious thick, pea soup, fog, obscuring the streets of Whitechapel. There also seemed to be a dismal atmosphere about the place, brought on by the sudden change from the mild and pleasant October to a new gloomy dampness. The fog had put a halt to Rayne's street entertaining, making her more determined to accept Buster Forbes' offer and play her fiddle in the music hall which had yet to be opened. Peggy, however, believed that he intended to gently persuade Rayne into taking him up on the offer. Buster had been extremely generous with her, not only allowing her to live rent-free in her newly set up grocery shop but he'd also supplied her with a varied supply of foodstuff, adamantly refusing her offer of an I owe you. Peggy was no fool when it came to the underhand dealings which took place in the Pool of London, Levi had enlightened her on the dangers of the pilfered supplies which passed from one poor man to another. He had claimed to be able to smell a haul of stolen goods from a mile away and would have nothing to do with them. Although Peggy didn't fully trust Buster Forbes, her choices were limited and part of her did feel sorry for him when she remembered how he'd suffered so badly at the hands of Edward Jackson.

Boredom had filled Rayne's head with daydreams of a life with August Miller, she prayed every night that he had not yet married her half-sister and that by some miracle he had fallen out of love with her. Letter after letter was written to him, she sat for hours composing poems, in the hope that it would make August recognise that she would be more suited as a wife; she told him of how she'd written her very own piece of music and how she'd love for him to visit her and her grandmother in Whitechapel to hear it. She also poured out her heart, saying how the death of Mr Levi had left them in the most appalling financial situation and how nightmares of the workhouse woke her up in a cold sweat every night. She advised him not to rush into marriage, adding that she was merely repeating her grandmother's sentiments, who had witnessed too many hasty marriages turning sour over the years. Rayne also wrote the briefest of letters to Eleanor but her words lacked the love and emotion commonplace from one sister to another and were, in fact, quite bleak in comparison to the jolly sentences she wrote to August. A dozen or more letters in total had been posted behind her grandmother's back, but there had been no response at all. Not understanding why he'd not replied to her, as the weeks passed by, Rayne grew more concerned that something untoward had happened to him.

Buster Forbes had been pulling out all the stops to set the wheels in motion for his new venture. Still not sure of how or what he intended to do in order to take revenge on the late Edward Jackson, his main aim at the moment was to convince Rayne to play her violin in his music hall and whilst she lined his pockets and stayed within his sights, he had plenty of time to plot a satisfying plan. An old disused warehouse in Commercial Street, just a stone's throw away from his office, appeared to be the ideal place in which to accommodate his music hall, a busy area, overcrowded with the sailors and dockers from the Pool of London and near to Whitechapel Street, where the menfolk would head for to unwind and fill their bellies after docking. It was also situated near enough for the womenfolk of the East End to flock to for an afternoon's entertainment. With her huge innocent eyes and her sweet untouched appearance, Rayne Jackson would be sure to mesmerize the brawny men as she glided her bow, producing sweet, angelic tunes or catchy jigs to keep the men's feet tapping. Already deciding to offer the prestigious role of music hall manager to Tommy Kettle, it was merely a way in which Buster could keep all of his options open. Knowing how Tommy would do anything to improve his relationship with Rayne, Buster couldn't help smiling to himself as wicked thoughts filtered through his devious mind; how Edward Jackson would be squirming in his grave, he considered, if only he knew how acquainted he was becoming to his precious daughter.

As the two workmen were engrossed in painting the shop front of the pawnbroker's, transforming its drab grey exterior into a fresh blue one, Buster Forbes arrived to offer his compliments and give Peggy more provisions to sell; this time it was a crate of tea leaves along with the suggestion that perhaps they should be the first to taste the fragrant leaves.

"I want to witness my name being painted for the world to view first, Mr Forbes, if you don't have no objections!" voiced Peggy, feeling annoyed that Buster had shown up at such an inappropriate time.

"And what is Mrs Bow's new empire ter be called?"

"*Peggy's Grocery*; that's what! Nothing fancy because folk around here prefer things plain and down to earth!"

"It sounds like a welcoming name ter me, Mrs Bow!"

"Well, it's a good job I've got your approval since I'm only the leaseholder!"

"Who knows Mrs Bow, one day every brick might 'ave yer name stamped on it! Now, where's that talented granddaughter hiding 'erself then? Don't tell me she's out in this smog playing 'er fiddle!"

"Course she's not, Mr Forbes, what sort of grandmother d'you take me for? Rayne is the apple of my eye and don't you ever let that slip your mind, Mr Forbes, because lease or no lease, Rayne comes first and if I even get a whiff of anything fishy going on...well, let's just say, it will be at your loss! She is *nothing* at all like her father, Mr Forbes!"

Buster's jaw dropped, as Peggy's words winded him. He was dumbstruck and Peggy knew it.

"You see, Mr Forbes, I'm no newcomer to Whitechapel! In fact, up until I was widowed and left stranded with my baby daughter in arms, who is none other than, Edward Jackson's widow, Whitechapel was my home! I thought your name rang a bell the second you introduced yourself. Those fancy togs and your wads of money don't wash with me, Buster Forbes, it was a terrible thing that my late son in law did to you but that was in the past and he's likely getting his comeuppance now in the next life, so if you've any notions of getting your own back, by mistreating my family, I suggest that you seriously think again!"

Buster chuckled loudly, "Mrs Bow, you're a real diamond, I can tell! What d'you take me for? I wasn't even aware ov your connection wiv Edward Jackson 'til a recent conversation I 'ad wiv Tommy Kettle, an' it was a *very* recent chat! Nah! Mrs Bow, yer barking up the wrong tree! I'm a businessman an' aim ter make a small fortune wiv the 'elp of yer granddaughter's talent! She'll make a few bob an' all, an' it will beat 'anging' 'round the streets in all weather, not ter mention the danger ov it! Rayne is a sweet girl, an' I wouldn't do a thing ter hurt 'er, Mrs Bow. Trust me! Edward Jackson doesn't even take up space in me head an' hasn't done fer years!"

Peggy gave him a long hard stare, wondering if he should be trusted. She doubted it, but for the time being she had little choice; she would just have to be extra vigilant and have eyes in the back of her head, she concluded.

"Very well, then, Mr Forbes, but don't for one minute think me to be a silly old woman who's lost her wits! Now if we're all to be in each other's lives you'd best call me Peggy; after all, it's written above the shop now, as bold as brass!"

Buster relaxed a little, feeling he'd convinced her of his honest intentions. "That suits me well enough, an' you should call me Buster! Now, are we gonna sup that tea? Perhaps Rayne could boil the water if she's about?"

Summoned by her grandmother, Rayne quickly hid her half-written love poems under her mattress and hurried downstairs to prepare the tea. Having a higher opinion of Buster than that of Peggy's, Rayne sensed that it would be to her advantage to have such an influential character on her side if she was going to become a successful and famous musician. It would also help her to win the love of August Miller and maybe even make him take more notice of her. Buster Forbes had a certain charisma about him, she pondered as she sat opposite him in the compact back parlour; always turned out in the finest quality and smartest clothing, he carried his bulky weight well, appearing powerful and untouchable to the copious scoundrels who roamed the streets of Whitechapel and behaved in a refined and charming way when the need arose. Rayne knew she'd be safe with him at her side. He complimented the tea as he swirled it around inside his mouth in a noisy fashion, commenting how its perfection was due to the way it had been skilfully prepared by Rayne. Peggy tutted and shook her head, annoyed by Buster Forbes' ridiculous praise.

"Oh yes, Buster, it is, *indeed*, a skill to brew a pot of Rosie Lee!"

Buster grinned and turned his attention to Rayne.

"I've found the perfect property fer our impending project, Rayne! I intend to 'ave one of the ware'ouses down Commercial Street, converted inter the fanciest music 'all this side of the river; we will become a beacon fer all them homesick sailors an' dockers alike! An' what's more, I'm gonna pay Tommy Kettle ter manage the place! What d'yer say 'bout that then?"

"Tommy Kettle is a good lad, one to be trusted!" declared Peggy.

Rayne giggled, "I'm surprised he even accepted the job after I turned down his marriage proposal! I would have thought he'd prefer to stay clear of me!"

"I've yet ter ask 'im, Rayne, but reckon it's better ter 'ave a loyal friend, who worships the ground yer walk on, looking after yer interests rather than some cocky little advantage taker!"

"For once I agree with you Mr Forbes!" commented Peggy.

"So, what d'yer reckon then, Miss Jackson? Does me offer sound tempting enough?"

Rayne had learnt a great deal during her three years in the East End and she was no longer a timid upper-class girl, afraid to speak her mind, neither was she intimidated by the likes of tyrants like Buster Forbes and felt sure that she could twist him around her little finger to get her own way. She had one aim in life and that was to make August Miller love her, no matter what or who stood in her path.

"Well so far, Mr Forbes..."

"Come on now ladies, didn't we just agree ter be on first name terms? What sort ov lasses am I dealing wiv 'ere?"

"Oh, very well, Buster," stated Rayne, confidently, "but, your offer holds nothing to tempt me! Don't presume that you can use my musical talent and my youthful looks, only to dump me in the gutter once you've made your fortune! I want at least eighty per cent of what my audience pay!"

Buster's eyes opened wide, "Oh, *Grandmother Peggy!* Hold the Rosie Lee...Reckon I might just choke ter death on it!" he expressed, laughing uncontrollably. "That's some shrewd granddaughter you've raised there!"

"I don't see anything wrong! Why shouldn't she have eighty per cent? She'll bring crowds into your establishment and no doubt you have many other ways and ideas up your sleeve to drain their pockets. Rayne will be your star attraction!"

"Don't be ridiculous, Peggy, these are dockers an' sailors! Men who've travelled the high seas and seen more than the likes of the entertainers who plague the streets of Whitechapel! As much as I'm sure they'll love the little *fiddle girl*, and at the risk of not embarrassing you, Peggy, those men will be hungry for an eye full and a feel of a real woman, if yer gets me meaning?"

"Well, Mr Forbes, if you think, for one minute, that I'm going to work side by side with common whores, you have chosen the wrong '*fiddle girl*'!" stressed Rayne.

"Quite right too!" added Peggy, proudly.

Already having had enough of the two females, Buster gulped down his tea, anxious to leave.

"Don't worry, Rayne, I've got everything planned out an' yer won't even 'ave ter utter a word ter one ov them common whores! Leave it ter me. I'll be in touch! Thanks fer the Rosie Lee, ladies!"

Leaving Peggy red-faced and Rayne deep in thought, Buster Forbes replaced his hat and sauntered out of the parlour.

# CHAPTER EIGHT

An early morning thunderstorm had woken Eleanor and for a few minutes, she oddly remembered the far off days when she and Tilly had slept on the river bank. Overwhelmed by her gloomy memories, she snuggled up closely to August, taking comfort in the sound of his gentle breathing and the familiar scent of his skin. The sound of young Felicity's cries echoed throughout the house; she was likely terrified by the thunder, which now clapped loudly, directly above Paradise Street. It had only been two weeks ago that they'd held a small birthday celebration to mark her first year. What a year it had been thought Eleanor, not just for her but for so many of the people in her life.

*"Tee, Tee!"* Felicity called out, in between her heartbreaking sobs. Eleanor wondered why Tilly was taking so long to comfort the infant, but decided to remain beneath the warmth of the blankets for a little longer before she went to investigate. Tilly had proved to be the perfect nanny for Felicity, giving Wilma complete peace of mind as she helped Austin to expand their business. With Winifred's skills and her strong desire to continue sewing, even though August had suggested that she should take life easy now after a lifetime of hard work, Wilma had decided to expand Hyde&Son into two stores; one of

which would cater for the female inhabitants of Oxford. With herself, Winifred and Rosa being such proficient seamstresses, it seemed like an obvious opportunity not to be overlooked and since she was now the proud mother to a daughter it would be a sound investment for Felicity's future too.

The chanting calls of Felicity had stopped, much to the relief of Eleanor. She never felt as safe as when she was indulging every moment alongside August before the new day had begun. He would always rise half an hour before her to light the fire in their room, put the small pan of water on to boil and make tea for them both. Eleanor considered it to be the best part of the day. She had August completely to herself and it was generally peaceful as the house slept and she relished in his attentiveness. He was the perfect husband, considered Eleanor and although they'd only been married for three months, she couldn't foresee a day when their relationship would be anything other than loving and caring. She would often cry tears of happiness when she was wrapped in his protecting arms, feeling an overwhelming sense of security, never before experienced in her life. She felt extra emotional on this day and seemed to have lost her usual morning energy. She also realised that there had been no sign of her curse for two months; the thought of a baby threw her into a state of muddled confusion and she wasn't too sure that August would be pleased either. He'd yet to ever bring up the subject and on the occasion when Winifred and her grandmother had teased that she might be carrying a baby in her belly, August had simply laughed it off as though it was a ridiculous and impossible assumption. A baby would also be quite inconvenient, pondered Eleanor. August was working every morning with Mr Hyde and writing for at least six hours every day and she was busy with young Charles all day and helping Tilly out when Felicity became too much of a handful. She had already developed a love for smacking the piano keys, with her small chubby hands, much to the annoyance of Charles who had threatened to banish her to the far end of the garden when it was time for his piano lessons, rather than put up with her constant screaming to accompany him.

"You're a thousand miles away this morning, my darling!" uttered August, as he climbed back into bed.

Eleanor had been so deep in her thoughts that she'd not even noticed August lighting the fire and making the tea. She smiled affectionately at him.

"My darling husband, how much I love you, you will never know!" Her voice was low and shaky and August immediately noticed her watery eyes.

He took her in his arms, his firm muscular body

resting against her soft curves.

"What is it my beautiful Eleanor? What troubles you on this brand new day?"

Eleanor swallowed the painful lump which had become lodged in her throat, "I'm not sure, August, I just feel a little tearful today and I can't think of any reason for it!"

August gently kissed her, small light pecks, upon her neck and cheek before finding her pretty, inviting lips.

"Come with me today, I'm going over to East Hanwell to check that Ma and your grandmother didn't leave any of their belongings behind before the new tenants move in, it will make a change and I'd love your company. We'll leave after luncheon so the day won't be too disrupted. What do you say?"

Eleanor liked the idea; it would make a pleasant change to go out for the afternoon even though the January weather was decidedly harsh at present.

"Alright then, I'll make us some sandwiches for the journey...we can leave earlier and be home before sunset!"

"Now why didn't I think of that!"

"Because you are the romantic author and I'm a practical girl!" giggled Eleanor, already feeling her spirits lifting.

They set off at midday after Winifred had cautiously disclosed her secret hiding place where she kept her memory box and requesting that Eleanor might sweep the floor before the final closing of the cottage, not wanting the new tenants to consider her anything other than a meticulously clean and tidy woman. Both August and Eleanor found her request amusing, knowing how fussy she was when it came to housework.

The air was fresh and pleasantly crisp as the sun shone brightly across the winter scenery. Eleanor wrapped the woollen blanket around both their bodies, feeling snug as she squeezed her body as close as possible to August's.

"Do you remember our first journey together to East Hanwell?" she asked.

August looked puzzled, "No!" he declared, "I don't believe I do!"

"August Miller! You are the worst teaser ever!" Laughing out loud, August quickly planted a kiss on her cheek. "How could I forget one of the best days of my life?" he added.

"Do you think your ma is sad that someone new is to occupy her cottage; it seems so final now doesn't it? I hope she won't suddenly decide that she wants to return to East Hanwell!"

"No, she loves her new life living next door to us, just as your grandmother does, and they've both become so quickly attached to everyone...it sometimes feels as though we've all been one happy family for years!"

"That's true," agreed Eleanor, "and young

Felicity and Charles adore them too!"
"They are like two new grandmothers fussing over them," added August, "which is a bonus since Mr Hyde is an orphan and Mrs Hyde seemed to have lost contact with her family when she married him. He told me how her parents never considered him a suitable husband and believed that Wilma was marrying beneath her social status!"

"I know, she told Tilly and me the same, but anyone can see that they are the perfect match and are devoted to each other!"

"I wonder how many hearts have been broken because of the social class!" exclaimed August annoyingly.

"You should write a book about such topics, August, a story to shock the world!"

"I might if I could guarantee it being published, but which publisher would want to risk ruin by associating with such an outlandish author!"

"Oh look, I can see the smoke coming from East Hanwell's chimnies!" declared Eleanor, excitedly.

"This young mare is twice as fast as old Duke used to be!" stated August as he steered the wagon off the main track and into the quiet hamlet.

A handful of children all warmly adorned with scarves, hats and mittens, were out playing; the girls skipping over an old rope and young boys still taking part in conker fights. All activities suddenly came to a halt as the sound of the wagon wheels drew closer.

"Look! It's August Miller and his pretty wife!" exclaimed a couple of the girls.

August emptied his pockets, and handed the oldest looking lad the sweets he'd bought for them, "Here you go, make sure you share these out fairly now, young man!"

A loud chorus of 'thank you' erupted from every well-mannered child as their eyes lit up and they licked their lips in anticipation of the sweet treats.

Eleanor smiled proudly as she watched her husband interact with the youngsters before helping her down from the wagon.

"The children love you August!"

"Hmmm, I think they love what's in my pocket! Come on, let's go and hunt for Ma's secret hiding place... and pray that she's not sent us on a wild goose chase! "

"Third shelf in the pantry to the left, is what she told me!"

"Mmm, she gave me the same location," confirmed August.

August lifted the latch of the front door already sensing that some of the neighbours would already have had a look around the place in his mother's absence. Eleanor immediately noticed the pile of letters that had been neatly stacked on the table.

"How strange," uttered August, "Ma seldom receives any post, and I've informed everyone who I correspond with of my new address." They were suddenly hit by a pungent musty smell emanating from within the tiny cottage which now seemed even smaller than August remembered it. The Hyde's house in Paradise was like a palace compared to the humble dwelling he'd grown up in.

Every single letter was written in the same handwriting and postmarked from London and everyone was addressed to Mr A. Miller, except for one which was for Miss E. Whitlock. A total of fifteen in all, leaving August quite baffled as to why there were so many.

"They must be from your old housekeeper, Mr Levi and your half-sister!" he announced, as he hastily flicked through the unopened envelopes. "We'll read them when we get home, otherwise it will be nightfall by the time we've gone through them!"

"It seems an awful lot; what if it's bad news or they require your urgent attention!"

"And what if we didn't visit East Hanwell today?"

"I suppose," mumbled Eleanor, her curiosity itching to read their contents. "I'll sweep the floor, as I promised your ma I would and you go and look for her special box. The sooner we finish the sooner we can be home again!"

August laughed out loud, knowing how

inquisitive his young wife was but glad that they would soon be leaving. The icy cold cottage seemed to have lost its old loving feel and resembled nothing more than a poor person's shelter, no modern conveniences, dirt floors and a pungent odour of mould since the stove had not been lit for months. He would be eternally grateful to Mr Hyde for liberating his mother and Eleanor's grandmother from the camouflaged squalor they had resided in and was convinced that their new home would be beneficial to their health, even though his ma continued to insist that the City was by far a dirty abode in comparison to the countryside.

Insisting that Eleanor began reading the letters on the journey back to Oxford, August soon regretted his suggestion. Starting with the oldest stamped postmark, Eleanor's voice soon trailed off into angry silence.
"My half-sister is clearly in love with you August! What on earth has given her such an absurd notion that she would make the perfect marriage match for you! You must have swamped her with the same charm which you overwhelmed me with!" Red-faced and fuming, Eleanor thrust the pile of letters into August's lap and turned to face the opposite direction.
"You're being childish, Ellie! I thought you trusted me! I gave your half-sister very little of my attention, in fact, I practically ran from her

persistent invitation to spend more time at Mr Levi's place! Trust me, Ellie, *please!*"

With hot tears streaming down her cold face, Eleanor suddenly felt the entire contents of her stomach being churned up and vomited. August pulled hard on the reins and attentively cleaned Eleanor's face with his handkerchief and wrapped her body in the blanket. She looked as pale as the winter sky, with not the slightest of colour in her cheeks.

"Let's get you home and into the warm, my darling!"

# CHAPTER NINE

By the time they'd arrived in Paradise Street, Eleanor's state of health had deteriorated; her complexion was a ghostly white and her lips pale, dark shadows had appeared beneath her eyes and as August carried her into the home, there was nothing in Eleanor's power to prevent her from being sick again. Tilly was quick to be at her side, insisting that August carried her up the three flights of stairs and put her into bed, while she brewed a pot of the medicinal tea which Prudence had taught her how to make. One spoon of tea leaves and a large sprig of dried sage together with ginger and honey.

"Drink this Ellie!" She encouraged as she sat on the edge of the bed.

Eleanor sipped the concoction whilst August was quick to kindle a roaring fire in the large attic room.

"Don't look so worried, August, I've witnessed Ellie looking in a far worse state than this; she will be fine once she's warmed through and got some of her grandmother's special brew inside her."

Eleanor was already looking better, the colour slowly returning to her cheeks.

"I shouldn't have taken her out to East Hanwell on such a cold day!" confessed August, guiltily. "The cottage was cold and damp too!"

"She'll be fine, August, I know my dear sister, she might look weak, but she's a tough fighter!" Eleanor let out a little giggle, "I'm not deaf, you know!"

"You see what I mean, August!" laughed Tilly. "Now I must go and see to Felicity; I left Charles in charge of her!"

"Thank you, Tilly!" expressed August, without diverting his concerned eyes from Eleanor.

"I'm sorry, my sweet darling!"

"Sorry for what August, you're not too blame for my funny turn!"

"Oh yes I am; I vowed to take good care of you for as long as I draw breath! We've only been married for three months and I've already subjected you to an afternoon in the freezing elements!"

Wrapping his arms around her, August gently stroked her silky hair as he lovingly kissed her, "I love you so much, Eleanor...My beautiful, Eleanor, you gave me quite a scare, you know!" At the back of her mind the pile of letters from Rayne Jackson continued to irritate Eleanor, she wanted so much to tell August of how she had a strong inclination that she was carrying their first baby but, felt so angry that Rayne Jackson had absurdly even considered it possible that she might become the future Mrs Miller; she was also furious with August, that he might have given Rayne the wrong impression. The joyful news which she held in her heart would only be soured if disclosed on this day when Rayne was so prominent and had caused Eleanor to feel quite unwell.

"It wasn't the weather, August, believe me, I've suffered nights in the ice-cold confines of the workhouse which nothing could compare to!"

August immediately shuddered as he always did whenever Eleanor mentioned the workhouse, he still found it too painful to imagine her spending two years in such a place and felt guilty for not having been more thorough in his search for her.

"It was the ghastly letters from my half-sister! And the thought that, for some ridiculous reason, she believes she could have a future with you at her side! The very thought of you loving another sends my heart into a dark and miserable place, August! I would sooner die than find out that you have such feelings for someone else!"

"*Ellie!* You are my world, my whole life and I am the happiest man alive because you have made me such! I swear to you, I did nothing to give Rayne Jackson any misleading ideas! And if it wasn't for the fact that she is your half-sister, I wouldn't have been so polite in expressing my opinion of her!"

Knowing that August was speaking nothing but the truth, Eleanor wrapped her arms around his warm neck and snuggled up close to him, trying to hide her tearful eyes.

"Oh August, I really don't feel any joy at the thought of meeting my half-sister! Does that make me sound mean and heartless?"

After a moment of contemplation, August replied, "No, my darling, certainly not! You and she have the same father but, your blood ties and feminine instinct may be presenting strong messages. You must go with what your heart dictates, my love."

"I couldn't agree more...and besides, I never really felt any kind of strong bond with my father, not as I did with my dear mamma, God rest her poor tormented soul! He was barely even part of my life, and as I see it, he put more burdens on my poor mamma than she could bear, causing her to become so depressed that her only escape, was to end her life!" Breaking down into tears again, August held her securely, knowing that whatever he said wouldn't ease her pain.

They ate supper in their room that night, with August informing the rest of the anxious household that even though Eleanor had made a swift recovery he'd insisted she was to have complete rest and a good night's sleep, but his main purpose was so that they could go through the pile of letters together and reply to Rayne Jackson, informing her that they were now happily married and living extremely busy lives which would mean that a journey to Whitechapel in the foreseeable future would be completely out of the question.

"The letter will have to come from you, Ellie," insisted August, as they finally finished reading the pages, infused with sentiments of love and poetry. Rayne had poured out her heartfelt emotions to August upon every sweet, perfume scented, page. The letter to Eleanor, though, could have been penned from a different person; it was without feeling and maliciously stated how Rayne believed that Beatrice Whitlock was to blame for every misfortune which had occurred during the last two decades and how it was inevitable that Eleanor was proving to be an exact copy of her late mother and trying to steel August Miller away from where he truly belonged, by her side. She wrote of their spirits being perfectly matched since they were artistically inclined and appreciated the romance of life which Eleanor would fail to understand since she was a common, illegitimate woman without refinement or pure breeding. She also mentioned how August had gone out of his way to have his true feelings engraved on an expensive silver bracelet that he'd gifted to her. Rayne had written the short but powerful inscription in the letter, causing doubts to suddenly flood through Eleanor again and more tears to fall.

*"I will hold you in my heart until you are mine!"* cried Eleanor, her face red and streamed with tear trails. "It sounds just like the sort of words

you wrote in your book...sounds exactly like the romantic sentiments of August Miller! *Did you give her such a gift, August?* Please don't lie to me because the truth always exposes itself in the end, just look at my family and the consequences of year upon year of lies and deceit!"

August was as shocked as Eleanor, he had no idea as to what she was talking about and certainly hadn't given any gift to Rayne Jackson, let alone a romantically engraved bracelet.

"You have to believe me, my darling, I know nothing whatsoever of any damned engraved bracelet. I was in the company of Rayne, Peggy and the charming Mr Levi, for no more than a couple of hours, in which we spent eating supper and talking about my book and how I was searching for you, my beloved. Then, of course, when it came to light of the fact that you were the same Eleanor who Peggy often spoke of and that you were Rayne's half-sister, the entire conversation switched to trying to work out where you might have gone! I wasn't ever alone with Rayne, so to claim there is any kind of mutual bond between us is simply preposterous, and as for the bracelet, well, I'd say it's absolute madness!"

"Forgive me August, of course, I believe you, but this is just so upsetting for me! Imagine how you would react if another man was claiming that I had feelings for him!"

August stood up and began pacing the floor,

whilst rubbing his head with the flat of his hand. "We must nip this in the bud as quickly as possible, Ellie!" he declared, crossly.

"Or, we could just ignore these letters! If we'd not have gone to East Hanwell, we would never have discovered them, and I've also just realised that the last letter was postmarked in November. Perhaps she's overcome her little infatuation with you and given up. Does she know that we are married?"

"In my last letter to them, I simply informed them that I'd found you and of how we intended to marry!"

"Rayne must be informed that we are married and that you and your family left East Hanwell a while ago so she'll presume you haven't read her pile of letters. Maybe we could also inform her how delighted we are that we are expecting our first baby! It might dampen her burning heart!"

"We could I suppose, but supposing Peggy wants to get in touch on hearing such news...you know how women folk are when there's news of a baby! I thought you intended to be completely honest too, my darling. Didn't you just say how lies always become exposed?"

Eleanor sat silently staring up at August, her huge blue eyes causing August to swallow hard as he felt himself swimming within them.

*"What is it, Ellie?"* He hurriedly knelt in front of her, sensing a change in the ambience all of a sudden.

"It's not the way I'd planned to tell you, my darling, but I do believe I'm not fibbing!"
Lost for words, August gently placed his hand upon her belly, staring in disbelief.
"Do you mean that our baby is actually growing in here as we speak!" he declared, in a croaky voice.
Eleanor giggled, she'd never seen such a quizzical expression upon August's face before.
"I'm quite sure of it, but of course I need to see the doctor to be absolutely sure!"
"No, you don't need a doctor, you need my ma, she will be able to tell you!"
"*How?*"
"No idea, but she's diagnosed many a newlywed hamlet girl of such good news in her time! Oh, Eleanor, I didn't think it possible that I could be any happier! We are going to be a proper family! *Our first child!* Oh, my darling I love you more than my words can express!"
"August Miller! Lost for words? Goodness, that must be a first!" teased Eleanor, with tears of delight in her eyes.

# CHAPTER TEN

The gusty March winds almost blew Rayne
along Commercial Street; it was her second week
playing in the aptly named *Forbes Entertainment
Hall*, but there was far more going on behind its
doors than that of a typical music hall. Rayne,
however, tended to turn a blind eye to the
reports which Tommy insisted on sharing with
her and although she was quite sure that her
grandmother was all too aware of Buster Forbes'
seedy goings-on during the late hours, for the
sake of her increasingly thriving business and
Rayne's job, she feigned ignorance. Although
Rayne didn't like to admit it, Tommy Kettle now
appeared quite dashing in his expensive and
finely tailored suits which for a change were a
perfect fit. He had also undergone a professional
Italian hair cut and with his newly acquired
musk and patchouli cologne he left a pleasantly
scented trail behind him. It was clear that his
new image had been orchestrated by Buster
Forbes, but it was a clever business move.
Tommy's dapper image at the entrance to the
music hall enticed the womenfolk in and also
gave him a look of superiority which the
menfolk respected and looked up to and more
importantly, seemed to keep them behaving in a
civilised manner. Rayne was the most popular of
the entertainers; her music was sweet and she

was young, pretty and pleasing to the eye. She had already attracted a regular and attentive audience especially amongst the young men, who all seemed to harbour the same infatuation with Rayne, and lived in hope that she might take notice of them and fall head over heels in love with one fortunate lad. Having received a few lessons from Buster on how to conduct himself around the ladies, Tommy no longer behaved like the devoted puppy dog, beckoning to Rayne's every request and demand. He played it cool as if she was no different from any other lass in Whitechapel, but once a week he would suddenly present her with a single red rose, or a petite nosegay. He complimented her less and was often the last person to greet her when she came and left the music hall. Rayne had noticed his change and felt inwardly annoyed, especially as she also witnessed the accumulation of young women who attended the music hall with their mothers of an afternoon; their only intention to make eyes at the smart and handsome looking manager. On occasion, she had been tempted to march over to the silly smitten girls and announce to them that she could snap Tommy Kettle up in a second by a mere click of her fingers if she so desired.

In the few months since Mr Levi's passing, Buster had become well acquainted with Rayne and her grandmother. His preference for Peggy was tenfold to that of Rayne Jackson, who he considered a spoilt and stuck up young lass, and although insisting on giving the impression that she was just like any other Whitechapel girl, under her outer layer, she was as pretentious as her mother who, according to Peggy, refused to put a foot in Whitechapel. It was as clear as crystal that Peggy had grown up in the East End, even though she'd spent fifteen years in Oxford and had lived many years on Edward Jackson's family estate, but since she'd always been a housekeeper she viewed life through different eyes and the ways of the wealthy had skimmed over her veins, but never flowed through them.

Holding on to her hat as the strengthening winds threatened to send it soaring, Rayne's mind was preoccupied with thoughts of August Miller and of the letter which had arrived on the previous day, and which her grandmother had not shown her until breakfast that morning. The jubilation had shone like a beacon on a foggy night from her grandmamma's face, and as she disclosed how she'd heard from Mr Miller, Rayne felt a rush of giddy excitement as she assumed, that finally, August was intending to visit them. But, her euphoria was short-lived and as she listened to her grandmother announce that Eleanor and August had married five months ago and were now expecting their first child, Rayne was unable to swallow her mouth-full of breakfast and was struck by a combination of nausea and anger. She had snatched the letter from out of Peggy's hand, reading it twice before silently leaving the table and slamming the door behind her as she stormed out of the house.

Peggy had always been aware of Rayne's infatuation with August Miller and prayed that this news would put an end to her granddaughter's childish dreams. In her opinion, she would be far suited to a hard-working East End lad, someone like Tommy Kettle, perhaps, who thought the world of Rayne and would spend his life going out of his way to please her. Feeling as though her entire world had been sabotaged, Rayne was not content to let go of her dreams and believed strongly that August had made a huge mistake, but with a baby on the way, it felt as though history was repeating itself and just as her poor Pappa had been shackled to that harlot of a woman, Beatrice Whitlock, now her only love was caught in the same sticky web with her illegitimate half-sister who she already despised, even though she'd not even set eyes on her. She had to formulate a plan, she mused, and save August from a life of misery and prove to him that he rightfully belonged in her loving arms.

Having left home early and marched in anger for the entire journey, she'd arrived before Tommy had unlocked the music hall door, but knowing how he often slept in his tiny office, she sensed he was inside the building and caused a ruckus, by hammering her fists upon the door.

"Where's the bleedin' fire?" spat out Tommy as he yanked open the door, looking as though he'd only just woken up.

"Just let me in Tommy, I'm in a foul mood and I need to get some practise in before we open!" She marched over the threshold, aggressively nudging Tommy out of her way with her elbow.

"Just about to make a brew...fancy one? Might put yer flamin' temper out! Yer don't wanna be setting fire ter that sweet fiddle now, do yer!" Tommy had a smug look on his face, which only annoyed Rayne further.

"If I wasn't a well-mannered lady, Tommy Kettle, I'd tell you what you could do with your brew! Now kindly leave me alone! I have work to do and I'm sure Mr Forbes wouldn't like to hear how you've been hindering my warm-up!"

Tommy hated witnessing Rayne in such a mood and for a moment he allowed his new approach to give way,

"You know, I'd do anyfing for yer, Rayne, don't yer? Just say the word an' I'll pull out all the stops ter ease yer problems. I 'ope Mister Forbes ain't bin givin' yer an 'ard time, 'ope that jumped up cove ain't bin makin' no unreasonable demands on yer!"

Suddenly realising that it would be in her best interest to keep Tommy on her side, Rayne felt as though a spell had suddenly hit her; a brilliant idea magically sprung into her head; one which she would definitely need Tommy's help with to put into motion.

"No Tommy, it's nothing to do with Buster, but thank you for being such a caring friend. You've always been so sweet to me, Tommy." She gazed wistfully into his eyes as she spoke, causing him to feel a little awkward as his heart played a thunderous beat.

"Maybe we could spend some time together later, and I can tell you all about my problem. What d'you say, Tommy?"

Tongue-tied and with his hands breaking into a clammy sweat, Tommy could barely believe what he was hearing. Had his smart appearance and his new approach finally worked their magic on Rayne? Had he, at last, captured her heart and made her see him in a different light? He had never felt so excited and optimistic about their friendship. He warned himself to stay cool and allow *her* to set the pace.

"I'm a bit busy terday Rayne, but I could meet yer this evening; we could go ter the chophouse if yer like."

"I'd love to Tommy. It will make a pleasant change!"

Following Tommy through the thick blue haze of smoke, the aroma inside the chop'ouse reeked of a dozen assorted meals all merged into one and straightaway caused Rayne's stomach to rumble. He led her to the nearest vacant seat, which was more resemblant to a church pew than a comfy dining chair. Rayne's skirts trailed through the two inches of greasy sawdust but with her concentration solely focussed on how to launch her cunning plan and how to tempt Tommy into playing along with it, she didn't bother to avoid the large puddles of fat in her path.

Although it was a quiet time of the day, most of the seats were already occupied and men women and only a few fortunate children were all too busy filling their mouths to take notice of anything other than what was on their plates. Rayne, however, couldn't take her eyes from the billing post which was pasted on the wall in bold black print, advertising, Forbes Entertainment Hall, with the famous '*Covent garden, fiddle girl*' publicized as the number one attraction.

"Look, Tommy! I'm quite famous aren't I!"

"Yeah," he mumbled, as he tried to catch the waiter's attention.

"Did you know about this?" continued Rayne, proudly.

"Course I knows; it was me who pasted it ter the wall!"

The fact that Tommy was behind it somehow made it feel less important to Rayne, and she said no more on the subject.

"Now, what would yer like ter fill yer sweet belly wiv? I'm gonna 'ave sausage an' mash cos I know they's right tasty, but feel free ter choose anything else, Rayne, no matter what the cost is!"

After glancing at the roughly written and misspelt chalkboard, Rayne decided to have the same as Tommy.

"This makes a nice change, don't yer reckon, Rayne? A bit like old times when you an' me first met!"

"Except that you never brought me here in those days, Tommy!"

"Well, I'm no longer that scruffy docker, Rayne. I've moved up in the world thanks ter Mister Forbes. Reckon 'e's done us both a favour!"

"I'm sure he's making a tidy sum too, Tommy! That man seems to have his finger in every pie around the East End, and not every one of those pies is as 'above board' like the sweet and innocent music hall!"

"Yer don't 'ave ter tell me that, Rayne! I've bin doing jobs fer Forbes since I were a schoolboy. Me eyes 'ave seen a fair bit ov 'is so-called pies!"

"Dear Tommy, you are such a good friend to me and I'm sorry that we ever had to fall out."

"D'yer reckon we could be more than just friends, one day Rayne! Yer must know 'ow much I love yer!"

Rayne felt tense and quite sickened at the thought of being more than just Tommy's friend. In her mind, he wasn't even that. He was a lovesick fool and she intended to take full advantage of his weakness to catch the man of her dreams and the man who she knew was born to be at her side."

"Oh Tommy, you've made me blush! You are a sweetie!"

As the two plates of food were noisily put down in front of them, Tommy felt warmed and a little hopeful by Rayne's words.

"Mmm, this looks delicious, Tommy, let's eat; I'm ravenous!"

With a twinkle in his eye, Tommy smiled lovingly at Rayne. He looked around him and hoped that everyone would witness the pretty lass who he was dining with.

Fifteen minutes later and with their hunger satisfied, Rayne suddenly broke down into gentle sobs, as she masked her face with her palms.

"What's wrong, Rayne...Oh me darlin', what's 'appened? Are yer feelin' sick?" The look of genuine concern was immediately etched upon Tommy's face as he sat awkwardly, not sure of how to respond.

"Talk ter me Rayne, tell me what's bovvering yer, me darlin'! Is it Forbes? I 'ope 'e ain't bin miss treatin' yer?"

"Oh no, Tommy! Mr Forbes is a *true* gentleman. It's my half-sister!"

"Yer 'alf-sister?" repeated Tommy, looking

confused.

"Yes, Tommy, she refuses to see me, or even write to me! In fact, she probably denies that I even exist!"

"But I always fought it were you that didn't want ter 'ave anyfing ter do wiv, Eleanor!"

"Oh, Tommy, you even remembered her name...you really do care for me!"

"Ov course I do, yer should know that, Rayne. I'd do anyfing for yer!"

His statement was like music to Rayne's ears and she knew that she had Tommy Kettle just where she wanted him.

"Can we leave, Tommy, I feel I'm embarrassing you by making such a spectacle of myself in public!"

"Sure we can, but I don't reckon anyone's paying much attention to us, 'specially since them women just stepped over the threshold!"

Rayne glanced toward the entrance where three, provocatively attired and hideously painted women had already begun to flaunt themselves to the menfolk, who were unable to lower their gaze.

"How about a sweet dessert, sir?" tempted the trio of harlots, causing a heated buzz amongst the patrons.

Spontaneously taking hold of Rayne's arm, Tommy led her out of the chophouse and into the bustling Street.

# CHAPTER ELEVEN

They meandered through the, now crowded, Whitechapel. The high wind had not let up and as it whistled through every side street, forcing any conversation to be yelled out above it, Rayne knew that she could not voice her proposed plan to Tommy in such conditions. Suddenly halting and placing her hand over her gaping mouth she dramatically exclaimed how she'd forgotten to bring her violin with her and how it was badly in need of polishing and tuning before the following day's performance. Tommy was reluctant to return to the music hall at this time of day. The evening entertainment would not yet have begun and with the building being practically empty, he was considering Rayne's reputation, should anyone notice them returning. Like a spoilt child, Rayne protested, knowing how easy she could persuade Tommy.

"Can't yer sort out yer fiddle termorro'?" he pleaded. "Surely another day won't make no difference!"

"Oh, but it will, sweet Tommy, I owe it to dear old Uncle Levi to keep his fiddle in immaculate condition and if I don't tune it before tomorrow I'm afraid my music will sound more like a wild catfight, and then what will Mr Forbes say when the audience demand their money back?"

Looking troubled, Tommy knew that he was left

with little choice other than to escort Rayne back to Commercial Street.

Her dressing room was deep in the bowels of the old building; previously a storage room when it was a warehouse, there were no windows to it and it was also a fair distance from the stage and main hall. Only Rayne held the key and had refused to share her dressing room with any other performer, even when she was not performing or on the premises during the evenings. She couldn't think of anything worse than allowing one of the lewd women entertainers to share her personal space.

Stopping briefly to light a lantern, Tommy led the way, illuminating the three flights of well-trodden stone steps and constantly reminding Rayne to tread carefully.

"Tommy, I've been up and down these old steps so many times that I could do it in my sleep!"

"But yer ain't used ter it being so dark are yer?"

"Of course I am Tommy, I quite often leave when it's dark, but I'm not going to argue with you, I know you just care about me Tommy and I can't tell you how thrilled that makes me feel!"

Tommy's heart skipped a beat as he spoke over his shoulder, "Give me the chance, Rayne and I'd be 'appy ter spend the rest ov me life carin' for yer!"

"Oh sweet Tommy, now is neither the time nor the place to discuss such a subject and besides, I don't think I could settle into any such romance until I have been united with my dear half-sister. I feel as though my whole body is yearning to meet her! She's my dear pappa's flesh and blood too, you know!"

"Well, it's the first time me ears 'ave listened ter anyfing nice 'bout yer 'alf-sister springing from yer spout, Rayne! What's changed yer mind all ov a sudden?"

They arrived outside of Rayne's dressing room, "Come inside, Tommy, we can talk in private and I can tell you all about my plan and *your* part in it…you did say that you'd do anything for me, didn't you, Tommy?" Rayne looked deep into Tommy's eyes as she took hold of his arm, gently enticing him into her room. An inner thrill consumed Tommy's entire body as he warned himself not to do anything rash which might anger Rayne and change the kind way she was treating him.

"I shouldn't be alone wiv yer Rayne. It ain't right!"

"Don't be silly, Tommy! I trust you, and I know you'd never do anything to harm me! Come on, nobody will ever find out!"

Tommy was easily persuaded and sat nervously opposite Rayne in her dressing room. He turned the lantern up, hoping that a brightly illuminated room might help dampen his overpowering feelings of passion. He sat awkwardly on a small cupboard while Rayne flung herself down upon the armchair. There was little else in the stark, cold room, a rusty framed, looking glass hung from one wall and a rough sketch of a country landscape in a cracked frame from another. A few dead posies, gifted from Rayne's many admirers were scattered about the stone floor in empty jam jars, emitting an unpleasant, mildewy odour.

"I know it might look as though I've had a sudden change of heart, where my half-sister is concerned, Tommy, but you must remember that when you heard my bitter and spiteful comments about dear Eleanor, I was deeply affected by the sudden passing of my Pappa, God rest his soul, and it was only natural for me to be so harsh. I have since grown up and desperately need the love and support of an older sister, even if she is just a half-sister. She has lost her mother too, and since my mother doesn't care tuppence about me anymore I feel we will take comfort in each other's love and care. Do you understand, sweet Tommy?"

"Hmmm, reckon I do, but I don't know what yer think I can do ter 'elp! I ain't got no magic wand!"

"Oh, Tommy, you are such a darling!" she declared as she purposely pulled off her bonnet allowing her hair to fall free from its pins.

Tommy couldn't take his eyes off her as he gawked at her silky dark hair cascading over her shoulders. She took a large handful of it and sat twisting it, teasingly between her fingers as she spoke.

"You see, Tommy, it's not as though I haven't tried my best to reach out to her. I've lost count as to how many letters I've written, only to receive one nasty reply in which she literally told me to leave her alone. I am that worried about her, Tommy; sometimes I can't sleep at night for fear of never meeting dear Eleanor!"

"So did she and that cove, August Miller, not get tergether then?"

"I don't think they did, Tommy, something definitely went wrong with that *great romance*. August wrote to my grandmother and told her that he intended to marry another. So I doubt they have any kind of relationship at all now. But I do know where she lives, though, but fear she could be living in misery; maybe she's even being held against her will...who knows, Tommy, but my heart tells me that she is in desperate need of my intervention and my instincts tell me that my poor half-sister is in terrible trouble!"

A spark lit up Tommy's pale blue eyes, "Why don't you an' me go ter Oxf'rd an' call on 'er!"

"Don't be so ridiculous Tommy! If my theory is right, she will not be allowed to receive callers or she might simply refuse to see me! No, we have to steal her away from Oxford and that's where you come into it, sweet Tommy! If you could somehow bring her to this very room, it would allow me to pour my heart out to her and explain how I wish to help her and be like a real sister to her. She might even end up working alongside me, Tommy! Grandmamma informs me that she is an excellent pianist! Imagine how pleased Buster will be to have a beautiful sister act playing here!"

The look of shock hadn't left Tommy's face as he sat with his mouth gaping.

"Oh say something, Tommy! You look like an old river bloater!"

"D'yer mean that yer wants me ter kidnap 'er?"

"*Yes, Tommy*, it's the only way. I'm quite sure she'll be glad, in the long run, and I will love you forever if you bring my darling sister to me!"

"Alright then, but I'll 'ave ter get someone else ter do it, I ain't cut out fer that sort ov crime!"

"It's not a crime, Tommy, but fair enough so long as you get someone trustworthy and by the way, not a word of this to anyone, especially my grandmother!"

"*Fine*, now let's get out ov 'ere afore the night crowds arrive!"

"Yes, Peggy will be wondering where I've got to. ...I hope she didn't save me any supper, I couldn't eat another mouthful!"

As she closed the dressing room door behind her, Tommy issued her with a curious look.

"Ain't her fergettin'?"

"Forgetting what, Tommy?"

"Yer fiddle ov course!"

"Oh, yes!" declared Rayne. "Silly me, I'm such a

scatterbrain!"

# CHAPTER TWELVE

It seemed that Winifred and Prudence were in hot competition as to who could knit and sew the most baby clothes; both euphoric at the prospect of becoming a grandmother and Great grandmother, Eleanor and August viewed the growing pile of tiny garments, and exchanged a furtive glance.

"Are you planning on selling at the Wednesday market again?" joked August.

"Don't be so daft son, a new baby can never have enough clothes to wear, now stop your criticising and come and sit down, poor little Ellie looks as though she needs to rest her legs! She shouldn't be walking so much in her condition!"

"Oh, I'm fine!" insisted Eleanor, as she followed orders and immediately sat on the nearest chair. "I've only walked from next door you know and I've spent my entire day sitting down, teaching young Master Charles. If truth be told, I'm yearning to go for a long stroll!"

"You're looking a bit pale, my darling," added Prudence, "and I wouldn't risk walking out in these high winds; you never know what might come flying through the sky and fall upon you! No, the best place is at home in the warm with your feet up! Isn't that right, Winifred?"

"Oh, yes, definitely! When baby Miller arrives,

you'll be rushed off your feet, so it would be wise to take advantage of these quiet days!" August and Eleanor only just managed to keep a serious face as they listened to the elderly, caring women's advice while waiting for Winifred to pour the afternoon tea. It was a regular gathering between the four of them at least three times a week, in between their time spent with Charles, who, if permitted, would spend every minute of the day in their company. He adored Winifred and Prudence and revelled in the attention they showered on him, not to mention the amount of delicious, cakes, pies and biscuits which were always offered in abundance. Winifred and Prudence also took great pleasure in taking care of Felicity; she was becoming quite a handful and now slept far less during the day. It gave Tilly a rest bite, but she inevitably spent her free time helping Rosa around the house or helping with Charles, insisting that Eleanor took an afternoon nap.

The afternoon was spent discussing August's latest novel which was near completion; a murder, mystery set in Whitechapel and as different to his last book as chalk was to cheese. Eleanor relished in hearing each completed chapter and Charles would constantly nag to hear the edited and less vivid retell the following day. He had since changed his mind about wishing to be a famous pianist and now dreamt of following in August's footsteps to become an

author. Winifred and Prudence spoke of Charles
and Felicity with great adoration and a twinkle
in their eyes; they loved spending time with the
young ones and it was indisputable at just how
happy they now appeared since moving into the
beautiful and modern, neighbouring house. It
was also a huge advantage having August and
Eleanor living next door to them. Often, of an
evening they would discuss how their life had
changed since leaving East Hanwell, both
having the same opinion that it had proved, by
far, to be the greatest change in their lives and
how they could never go back to the dull, old
ways.

*************

The relentless gales caused the smaller shipping
vessels to bash noisily against the quayside and
the wind to howl through the windows of the
Salty Dog inn, where the swollen wood hindered
their complete closure. Buster Forbes was sat
with his eyes and ears open wide to the drunken
banter, awaiting news of any interesting
shipments due to arrive. The last person he
expected to see was the suave looking, Tommy
Kettle. Garbed in his expensive working togs,
Buster felt immediately irritated that his young
employee had not changed into something more
suited to visit the filthy thieves' den. Tommy
failed to notice Buster, who was concealed in the
shadows, seated far from the brightly burning
fireplace. Tommy was obviously looking for

someone, mused Buster, as he watched with intrigue. Tommy Leaned against the bar, and appeared on edge as he turned his head in every direction, soon acknowledging none other than Sid Crewe, also known amongst his enemies as '*The Scavenger*'. A scrawny man in his late fifties, he appeared far older; his yellowish skin eroded by time and a life of crime and poverty. At first glance, nobody would consider him to be a threat, but he was one of Whitechapel's most ruthless and feared men. His buried eyes suddenly caught sight of Tommy Kettle and he sauntered towards him. Buster was completely absorbed but knew he'd have to remain glued to his seat if he didn't want to be discovered. He wondered what business Tommy could want with Sid who was notoriously known for causing folk to mysteriously disappear, never to be seen alive again; in many cases, their remains would be discovered by the mudlarks at low tide, days or weeks later. He felt a chill run through his body; he couldn't for the life of him think of any reason why Tommy would even endeavour any kind of association with the unscrupulous, Sid Crewe. The pair made their way to a side table, well away from any prying ears and eyes, but within good view, for Buster to observe and attempt to read their lips. He sniggered quietly to himself as Tommy pulled out a silver hip flask and topped Sid's tankard up. He'd have to keep an eye on Tommy Kettle, considered Buster, he was becoming too much like himself and if Tommy could afford to carry a silver hip flask around with him, he was likely to be fiddling with the music hall's books. Their meeting was brief, Tommy slyly handed Sid a scrap of paper before they shook hands and Tommy scurried out of the Salty Dog, his face tense and his stance awkward. Buster remained in his seat, with his watchful eye on Sid. They were enemies and had been rivals for more than a decade. Buster knew better than to interfere in his business, unless he wanted to end up with another scar to add to his collection, or worse, but he was desperate to know what was cooking between Sid and Tommy and wondered if Tommy was aware of how dangerous a man he was dealing with. Deciding to call on Tommy in the morning and run through the accounts, Buster left the Salty Dog with a feeling that curiosity was going to keep him awake all night long.

*************

It was late afternoon and as Tilly helped Rosa prepare the vegetables for the family's evening meal and Charles was following his father's instructions, preparing the dozens of terra cotta flower pots, ready for him to sow the annual seeds, Eleanor was in a deep sleep. The only sound to come from their attic room was that of August's nib scraping across the paper as every one of his thoughts was engulfed in the adventure he was bringing to life. The delicious aroma of roast beef floated up through the three flights of stairs, teasing August's senses and inducing him to include a mention of food into his writings. He glanced at Eleanor; she radiated beauty, even more so now that she was with child. August felt his heart overflowing with love for her. His ma had confirmed that Eleanor was expecting shortly after the disastrous day they'd spent in East Hanwell and later during that same month a special visit to Doctor Thompson verified the good news and he'd also announced to them that he predicted the baby to arrive in August, which had become a very special month to them both, for more reasons than one. August had briefly hinted that if the baby was a boy he should be named after him, but Eleanor believed her life would become far too confusing with another August in it. He felt his stomach rumble as he glanced at the clock; the light was fading and he decided to finish writing the chapter before lighting the lamps and waking Eleanor before supper.

"Shouldn't you be on your way next door by now Tilly?" reminded Rosa. "You'd better go and fetch Felicity before Mr and Mrs Hyde return, I don't want the meal to spoil!"
"You're right Rosa, by the time I've listened to everything Prudence and Winifred have to tell

me about Felicity's eventful afternoon with them, and I've drunk the mandatory cup of tea, the vegetables will be cooked to perfection!" laughed Tilly. "I'll sneak out quietly so that Master Charles won't insist on accompanying me, otherwise I'll not be back 'til midnight!" Rosa glanced out of the window, "He looks happy enough in the greenhouse; up to his elbows in soil though, but boys will be boys!" Tilly hung up her apron and quickly ran both hands over her head, making sure there were no loose strands of hair, but then decided she'd appear far more composed if she wore her bonnet. Rosa giggled, "Tilly! You're only popping next door!"

"But, you never know who you might bump into out on the street," she replied, with a wide smile. "Remember how Ellie bumped into August by chance when *she* was just popping to the pie shop!"

"Oh, you are such a romantic, Tilly! One day I'm sure *Mr Right* will come along and sweep you off your feet!"

"You too, Rosa! You are still young enough to fall in love again and marry *and* have a handful of beautiful children! They do say that love comes along when you least expect it!"

"Oh, Tilly, be off with you!"

Beneath the accumulating dark clouds, Tilly neither saw nor heard a single sound, until it was too late and the chloroform soaked rag seemed to suddenly spring from nowhere, sending her into instant oblivion. Sid Crewe's cumbersome accomplice effortlessly carried her to the awaiting rusty, black carriage causing Sid to grin with delight when he caught sight of the pretty young girl. Tommy Kettle had instructed Sid to keep it to himself that this pretty petticoat was no other than the fiddle girl's illegitimate half-sister, who she was desperate to meet. Considering it a rash and unnecessary way of meeting a family member, not to mention the price of three guineas that he was to receive on delivery, Sid furtively considered that there was more behind this little ploy than he'd been told. From now on he would keep an eye on that fiddle girl, he decided, maybe she wasn't as sweet and innocent as folk believed. While his accomplice sped from Paradise Street, heading towards the London Road, Sid mercilessly tied Tilly's hands behind her back and her ankles together before securing a filthy piece of rag tightly around her mouth.

"That should keep yer as quiet as a mouse, *Eleanor of Oxford!*" he sniggered, resting his mucky boots upon her body as she lay lifeless upon the grimy carriage floor.

With the greatest of urgency, Austin Hyde grabbed hold of his wife's arm just as she was about to cross the main thoroughfare to Paradise Street and into the path of the runaway carriage. The antiquated and badly driven carriage had caught his attention whilst Wilma had been preoccupied viewing the few costermongers barrows, who'd yet to retire for the day.

"What a *blithering* fool!" he bellowed, as he froze in shock, witnessing the speeding carriage disappear out of sight."

"That mad man could have run me over, if you weren't so vigilant, my darling!" cried Wilma, her face pale, all of a sudden.

"Are you quite alright, old girl?"

"A little shaken, but more shocked by the presence of such an uncouth vehicle on the streets of Oxford!"

"It's the first time I've ever seen such a rusty bucket on wheels in this vicinity!" admitted Austin. "And I hope it's the last!"

"Indeed!" agreed Wilma. "I pray it was merely a traveller who'd lost his bearings; now enough gawking, Austin, you know how irritated Rosa becomes if we're not home at least fifteen minutes before the evening meal is ready to be served!"

"Oh yes, how could I forget? I often wonder who are the employees and who are the masters under our roof!"

"Oh don't be so silly, Austin, we broke the mould with tradition when we married and it hasn't stopped since! We are all happy and everything ticks along like clockwork, and at the end of the day, it is you and I who own everything and are becoming wealthier with each passing year!"

"There speaks my shrewd business partner!" teased Austin.

"In six months we will be ready to open the ladies side of the business and then just you watch as our beautiful gowns fly off their hangers faster than we can make them! I don't know why we didn't venture into such a project before now, it's common knowledge that women spend far more on their clothing than men!"

"Because, my kind and thoughtful wife, you wanted me to have a suitable business to run!"

"Gosh, I'm ravenous; I can't wait to take the weight off my feet and enjoy a relaxing evening!"

As they stepped into the Vestibule the delicious aroma increased their hunger, Charles marched to greet his parents, at the same time donning his cap upon his head of curls.

"And where do you think you're off to, young man?" inquired Wilma as she hung up her day hat.

"I'm just going to tell Miss Tilly that it's time to come home! Rosa said that I should go and rescue her! She said that she's too polite to leave Mrs Miller and Mrs Whitlock and that dinner is almost ready!"

"Is Felicity still with the ladies, Charles?"
Charles chewed on his bottom lip as he nodded, hoping it wouldn't put his ma into a cross mood.

She stared at her son for a brief moment,
 "What have you been up to Charles! Your arms are filthy and it looks as though you have half the garden beneath your fingernails."
 "I've been doing some gardening for Pappa! He asked me to fill up all his pots with soil!"
Wilma issued Austin with a fiery look, "Oh did he indeed! Well, young man, you need to wash before dinner, so run along. I suppose I will have to go and bring Tilly and Felicity home!"
 "I'll go!" suggested Austin, "I doubt they'll have much to say to me!"
 "Oh don't you believe it, but at least I will have time to prepare for dinner, while you're away, and make sure this young gardener scrubs those disgusting fingernails!"

# CHAPTER THIRTEEN

Having given up on Tilly's prompt return from next door, Rosa hastily laid the dining table and the smaller kitchen table in readiness for, Eleanor, August and Tilly. Charles had been scrubbed clean by his unsympathetic mother who had also changed, anticipating a pleasant evening ahead, and now, as all eyes viewed the ticking grandfather clock, Rosa was fast becoming vexed over the meal losing its heat. The unmistakable voice of Felicity as she spoke in her sweet baby language, soon delighted everyone's ears and immediately transformed the strained atmosphere. It was, however, to be short-lived; Austin Hyde looked completely dumbfounded as he handed the chirpy infant to Wilma and declared in a worried voice that Tilly had never gone next door to collect Felicity. Everyone was suddenly masked by a look of shocked confusion. Eleanor and August were soon downstairs and informed of the bizarre events. Completely puzzled, they too could think of no reasonable reason why Tilly would have gone somewhere else, without mentioning it to Rosa.

Eleanor felt the sudden need to sit down, consumed by an awful shadow of darkness, her inner sense and her close bond with Tilly immediately told her that Tilly was in some kind of trouble. Wilma was the first to witness how pale she'd turned and ordered August to fetch a blanket for his shocked wife.

"Is it at all possible that today is one of Tilly's many significant memorial days, Ellie?" asked Mr Hyde, his brow still deeply furrowed, causing his eyes to almost disappear beneath his bushy eyebrows.

Eleanor was thinking the same thoughts; could it be the date that one of her parents had passed away? She wasn't sure; Tilly had never in the past commemorated such sad occasions. Had she met someone special and was meeting him in secret? She also pondered but knew that she would have told her if that were the case. She disclosed her thoughts to everyone and they all considered Eleanor's last theory to be the most likely scenario. Wilma suggested that perhaps she was seeing an older man or perhaps one who Eleanor and the rest of the household would warn her against.

"Do you mean a married man, Mrs Hyde?" uttered August.

"Sadly, that's exactly what I *do* mean! And What's more, knowing what a considerate young woman Tilly is, she would not have wanted to burden dear Ellie with such news, in her delicate condition!"

Eleanor was not convinced, it didn't make any sense, and she knew Tilly far better than anyone else. They were like sisters and had vowed to share everything, with no secrets and Eleanor was quite confident that she would have sensed if Tilly had fallen in love.

"I don't believe Tilly has a beau, Mrs Hyde and I'm sure if she did, I would have been the first to know! And why would she choose to meet him half an hour before our evening meal! No, that doesn't make any sense to me!"

"Love doesn't make sense though does it Ellie?" expressed Wilma, theatrically. "You should be the first to acknowledge that! A few precious moments on a street corner, a stolen minute at any time of day can be a treasure when two people are head over heels in love! And time inevitably slips by unnoticed during such romantic engagements!"

Austin Hyde coughed loudly, gaining his wife's immediate attention, "What is it Austin?"

"My dear, I know how much you love to devour all those romantic novels, but life isn't always like that!"

"I assure you it is, my dear!" snapped Wilma, belligerently, "but we women tend to remain romantic throughout our entire lives! Why Do you think that we spend our spare time engrossed in the pages of romance? It's because men become mundane and boring after they have caught their woman!"

Austin let out an embarrassed laugh, "My dear wife you make it sound as though we men go out fishing for their wives!"

Charles, who had been quiet since hearing the news of Tilly, suddenly spoke out with the most sensible and feasible suggestion of the evening, "Maybe Tilly went to buy a special present for Mrs Ellie since she's been feeling poorly; *they are like sisters*, and if Felicity was ill, I would want to buy her a present!"

In awe of Charles' sweet and level-headed statement, a sudden shift in how everyone had been thinking was brought about.

"There you go!" expressed Mr Hyde, proudly, "If you want sensible answers, just ask an eight-year-old! Their young minds have yet to be contaminated with love and romance!"

"I love *everyone* here!" Charles objected, "and I love Tilly and Grandma Miller and Grandma Whitlock!"

"Why don't we all eat, before the meal becomes stone cold. I'm sure Tilly will soon turn up bearing a gift for her dear sister!" announced Austin, suddenly feeling the need to satisfy his hunger and to dampen the needless crisis which was causing everyone to become overdramatic.

\*\*\*\*\*\*\*\*\*\*\*\*

Sid Crewe puffed away on his clay pipe spitting out bits of tobacco onto Tilly, now and again. He stuck his head out of the window where a glass panel had once kept out the cold wind. The eroded, milestone read fifteen miles to London. He pulled his collar up around his neck and swore at the biting wind which was freezing the side of his head, causing it to throb.

"For the bleedin' pittance I'm makin' fer delivering you, *Miss Eleanor*, I must be going soft in me old age!"

Tilly heard his words, her head felt foggy but she was quite certain that she had clearly heard the foul-mouthed man. She immediately closed her eyes again, praying that he'd not noticed her awake. She could feel the ropes, burning tightly against her skin and her mouth was dry and uncomfortable from the foul-tasting gag. As she went over the man's statement in her head she felt a little relieved knowing that he was merely an evil delivery man and would most likely not harm her. Her body suddenly jolted as the carriage rode over an obstacle on the road. Tilly released a muffled cry and made the mistake of opening her eyes. Sid Crewe's piercing beady eyes were like searing coals boring into Tilly. For a moment there was a strange silence as they seemed to weigh each other up.

"Bet yer wonderin' what's 'appened, ain't yer, Miss fancy *Eleanor!*"

Tilly blinked as she felt her heart thrashing against her rib cage and pulsating throughout her entire body. She had to stay composed, she coaxed herself.

"Some cove is right desperate ter meet yer, that's fer sure!" he stated, before cackling like a sick hyena. "Reckon it'll be 'bout 'alf an hour 'til I dispose of yer, *Miss Eleanor!*"

A deep pothole in the road suddenly caused the carriage to balance precariously on two wheels and for a brief moment the sound of falling nuts and bolts, together with the vehicle's increased rattling sound sent Tilly's heart racing, as the carriage appeared to be travelling faster than its old condition warranted. Sid Crewe guffawed loudly, amused, it would seem, by the look of fear upon Tilly's face.

"Don't yer likes a bit ov fun, *Miss Eleanor?*"

Tilly swallowed the bitter-tasting bile in her throat as she wondered how long it would take for her obnoxious kidnapper to realise that he'd snatched the wrong girl. She was glad though; such a rough and traumatic experience would be far too much for Eleanor to cope with in her present, fragile condition. She wondered who was behind the operation but already had a sneaky feeling that it must have something to do with Eleanor's vile half-sister. Eleanor had been heartbroken when she'd explained what had caused her to become so distraught on the day she and August had visited East Hanwell; everyone else had presumed it was due to the early days of her confinement, but she knew the truth. Eleanor was convinced that once she and August had replied to Rayne Jackson, telling her of their news, it would bring about an end to her unhealthy obsession with August. Although she'd agreed with Eleanor, solely to give her peace of mind, Tilly, however, harboured a fearful notion that it would take more than a letter to rid Rayne Jackson from their lives.

"Ain't no need ter look so bleedin' scared, it ain't me that wants anyfing ter do wiv yer. Oh no, there's a right 'andsom cove who hired me ter fetch yer, *Miss Eleanor*. Bloody shame is all I can say!" As usual, he let out another high pitched cackle before spitting out of the gaping window and yelling a mouthful of abuse at his accomplice, who failed to answer.

Tilly detested the sickening man and loathed the mocking way in which he kept saying, *'Miss Eleanor.'* The only comfort she took from the entire episode was that her dear sister was safe and sound in Paradise Street.

When the carriage finally came to a standstill, Sid Crewe didn't loosen her ropes or undo the overly tight gag. He winked his beady eye at Tilly, declaring repugnantly how he hoped his services wouldn't be needed again where she was concerned. Tilly sensed immediately that there was an evil and hidden message behind his declaration and couldn't wait to be separated from the cackling, scrawny man who appeared to be devoid of a heart. The carriage shook noisily as Sid Crewe's accomplice alighted, once again picking her up as though she was nothing more than a piece of hand luggage. Surrounded by dark shadows and the sound of copious voices, as Tilly strained her eyes to get a glimpse of where she was, a rough sack was suddenly pulled over her head. Her senses told her that she'd been taken off the street and into a building. She felt every step as the clumsy man carried her down endless flights of stairs. It wasn't just his footsteps she could hear, there were others with him; she could hear their breathing even though no words were exchanged. A few minutes later she felt the luxury of a padded cushion beneath her body and her instincts told her that she'd been delivered to her destination. Tilly sat nervously in silence, as the sudden realisation that her life could be in great danger dawned on her. With sweating hands and an overpowering feeling of nausea, she knew that if Rayne Jackson did turn out to be behind her kidnap, she might want her eliminated from the scene before attempting to lure August into her warped ploy. Would she know immediately that she wasn't Eleanor, deliberated Tilly, frantically; what would happen to her then? Would she be disposed of first, before Eleanor was then kidnapped? She could no longer think straight; infused with distressing thoughts, she was panic-stricken and petrified of the fate which awaited her.

# CHAPTER FOURTEEN

The sound of a door opening was followed by a female voice; a soft voice belonging to a young woman deduced Tilly, now more convinced than ever, that she was Eleanor's half-sister. Rayne stood nervously, staring at the figure slumped in her dressing room, armchair; Eleanor had the same petite figure as she had, mused Rayne, now overly curious to see what she looked like; Her grandmother had often said how pretty Eleanor Whitlock was, but then, being an old woman, she considered every girl under the age of twenty-five to be beautiful. The only time she'd ever laid eyes on her before was during the awful day in the office of Thornberry&Son; she'd taken little notice of her and that trollop, Beatrice Whitlock and with all the women so heavily veiled in their black mourning ensemble, it had been impossible to view their features.

"Do you know where you are?" she spontaneously asked, not realising that beneath the sack Tilly was also heavily gagged. "It won't do you *any* good to remain silent, you know *Eleanor!*"

If the situation wasn't so disturbing, Tilly would have liked to laugh out loud at her captives' stupidity.

"Very well, Eleanor, until you decide to speak,

you will remain in darkness."

Rayne stared hard at Tilly's belly; the mere thought that her darling, August's baby was growing before her very eyes angered her; she should be the woman to present August with a child, not this illegitimate guttersnipe, she mused spitefully.

There was a knock on the door; Tilly almost stopped breathing as she tried to hear the whispered conversation between Rayne and the man, but they soon left the room, leaving Tilly in silence once more.

"Are you sisters getting on well, me darlin'?" inquired Tommy. "Is she as nice as yer expected?"

"Oh, Tommy, you've got no idea, have you? These fragile situations must be taken slowly. I can't expect her to love me so soon after I've had her kidnapped!"

"Yeah, but yer rescued 'er from a miserable place didn't yer? She should be 'appy! I reckon once yer explains everything, you'll be like proper sisters, just like me own sisters; me ma says they are joined at the 'ip, on account ov 'em always being tergether!"

"Well, Tommy, I don't wish to be joined at the hip with *her!* She's yet to utter a single word to me!"

"So what does she look like, Rayne? Does she look like you? Bet she ain't as pretty!"

"Don't be such a dimwit, Tommy, we have

different mothers and besides, she's a mongrel!"
Tommy was shocked by her cold words.

"I've gotta go an' do me work, now! Reckon
Forbes might be down 'ere later; 'e was snooping
about early this morning an' asking me a load ov
odd questions an' 'e checked' the books an' all!"

"Heavens above, Tommy! What on earth have
you been up to?"

"Nought, I ain't bin up ter nought!" Rayne was
instantly alarmed by Tommy's raised voice and
his crimson face.

"Don't let him come down here to my dressing
room, Tommy! *Whatever you do*."

"An' just 'ow d'yer suggest I stop 'im? Knock
'im out?"

"You're being silly again, Tommy! But I know I
can trust you to keep my secret safe!" Quickly
giving him a peck on his cheek, Tommy was left
with the feeling that Rayne would soon be his
girl. He gazed in admiration of her as she
dashed back to her dressing room. He'd do
anything for her, he mused, she was like a bright
diamond compared to the other girls of
Whitechapel.

************

With everyone, apart from Charles, having
suddenly lost their appetite, Rosa hurriedly
made the coffee and as they all continued to
speculate on the possibilities of where Tilly
might have gone, August went next door to
invite his ma and Prudence to join them. His

mother often seemed to have a sixth sense and he prayed that she might come up with a more plausible explanation than anyone else had so far suggested. Whilst Eleanor had sat listening to everyone's thoughts and ideas, she was becoming increasingly concerned about Tilly. She knew her better than anyone, and after spending most of her childhood in the workhouse, Tilly had been left with a nervous and often anxious disposition. She loathed to go anywhere on her own and was happiest within the safety of the Hyde's beautiful home. Eleanor felt that it would be up to her and Rosa, maybe even August to initiate some matchmaking in the future and introduce Tilly to some suitable suitors. In fact, August already had a young man who he'd met whilst working in Hyde&Son, who he considered might have potential. Appearing tense, Winifred and Prudence were both well aware of the close and loving bond which Eleanor and Tilly shared and didn't wish Eleanor to be faced with any stress which might affect her delicate condition.

Time was getting on, and when Wilma insisted that Charles went to bed he was not prepared to retire without a protest, claiming he'd never be able to sleep until Tilly was home and safe. It was Eleanor who persuaded him, with the promise of a special treat in the morning instead of two hours of mathematics.

As they all sat around, sipping extra strong

coffee, deep in thought and unable to relax, it seemed that no matter how many times they went over Tilly's every last move and the sentences she'd spoken before walking out of the house, they ended up at square one without a single clue. Rosa had recalled how Tilly had seemed a little extra concerned about her appearance when she'd left, and how she'd jokingly commented that she could quite easily bump into someone, referring to how Eleanor had met August. Austin and Wilma were convinced that she was meeting a secret beau, but everyone else was unanimous in saying that it was out of the question and out of her character. Eleanor had stated how Tilly only had twenty minutes to spare, before the evening meal and was going to bring Felicity home to wash and change her. If she did meet someone it was definitely not pre-arranged. Tilly was a sensible, trustworthy young woman they all concluded, who would never just vanish of her own accord. Eleanor felt a sudden rush of goosebumps race across her skin and overcome with emotion, she could no longer stop her tears from falling.

*"Poor Tilly! She's in trouble! I know she is!"* Prudence was quick to wrap her arms around her granddaughter, "There, there, my darling, you mustn't upset yourself, think of that sweet baby! We will all put our heads together and find out what's happened to her."

"We should inform the police, Austin!" announced Wilma, to which August and Austin exchanged a quizzical look.

"*My sweet, dear!* We will be the laughing stock down at the police station, not to mention being reprimanded for wasting their precious time! It's hardly a crime when a servant goes missing for a few hours. And I know we don't consider her as a servant, but I'm afraid the police will and they'd fail to understand our eccentric way of life!"

August immediately, agreed with him, suggesting that if they couldn't come up with any leads themselves in the next twenty-four hours, they should hire a detective.

"There! *You see, Wilma!* Here speaks a young author who is writing his very own detective story! Maybe August has the mindset of a detective too!"

"This is not a time for jokes, Austin!" expressed Wilma, crossly. "Just look at poor Eleanor! She's devastated!"

\*\*\*\*\*\*\*\*\*\*\*

Rayne tiptoed from her bed and stood with her ear to the door of her grandmother's bedroom, relieved to hear her peaceful snoring. It was nearly eleven o'clock and not wanting to risk her half-sister dying of thirst during the night, as much as she feared the streets of Whitechapel at this hour, it was a sacrifice she felt obliged to make. She donned a huge black hooded cape, one she'd taken from Uncle Levi's old stock a couple of years ago; immediately seeing its advantages. She felt safe and protected when hidden beneath its oversized hood. Knowing where every creaking floorboard was situated, she gingerly avoided them as she crept downstairs and out through the front door of Peggy's Grocery. Keeping her slight body close to the shops and houses and with her head down, Rayne took large mannish paces as the sound of the brazen, women of the night and drunkards echoed through every dark alleyway. Whitechapel, after dark, transformed into another world; gone were all the familiar smiling faces of the costermongers and eager shop keepers, enticing customers into their premises; the sound of the copious children playing in the streets had disappeared only leaving behind the impoverished, filthy street urchins who huddled in shop doorways, either sleeping or begging for scraps of food or a farthing from every passer-by.

Unable to move from the position she'd been abandoned in, Tilly had spent the past few hours listening to the sound of distant music and crowds of cheering voices, deriving at the conclusion that she was being kept prisoner near to a place of entertainment. She wondered what everyone was doing back in Paradise Street and if anyone had witnessed her being stolen away by the villainous strangers. Were they out searching for her? She prayed hard in her heart that they were, and was now quite certain that she'd been brought to London. The sound of the key turning in the lock caused her to straighten her back, she felt the sudden increase in her pulse but at the same time was quite glad that her stagnant situation might be about to change. The terrifying thought that she might be nearing the end of her life had already distressed her more than a dozen times since her abduction, but she had succumbed to praying that, if it was to be the case, it would be implemented quickly and humanely.

"Hello, Eleanor! Are you still awake?"

Tilly shook her body in the chair, and, at last, it dawned on Rayne that her prisoner was unable to speak. She walked towards her and announced how she was about to remove her blindfold. Tilly swallowed, half expecting to be greeted by the sharp blade of a knife. The sack was gently removed and they stared curiously at each other. Tilly's immediate thoughts were of how young she appeared and how, if this was Eleanor's half-sister, Eleanor was by far the more beautiful of the two. Rayne could see no resemblance to her sister, which delighted her. Neither was she as pretty as her grandmother had insisted.

"I believe we are half-sisters!"

Their eyes met and held their gaze for a few

awkward seconds before Rayne struggled with the knot at the back of Tilly's head.

"If you are intending to scream when I remove this gag, you might as well know that we are in the basement of a noisy music hall, and won't be heard above the ruckus upstairs!"

At last, Tilly was set free from the excruciating gag and could breathe easy again. Her face felt tender and bruised. She desperately wanted to nurse it and wondered if Rayne was going to free her hands of their ropes too. She watched as Rayne poured out some water from a jug before placing the glass to Tilly's dry lips, allowing her to take small sips of the soothing liquid. Water had never tasted so good and she couldn't swallow it fast enough.

"What are you going to do with me?" asked Tilly, in a small voice as soon as she'd emptied the glass.

"Well, that all depends on how cooperative you decide to be, Eleanor!"

"Surely you don't mean to harm me! We're flesh and blood remember!"

Rayne squinted her eyes as she issued Tilly with a menacing look, "I'm sure there are more than a handful of our father's *little bastard* children running around in this world, but your slut of a mother was the only woman who managed to keep her claws firmly dug into him! You mean nothing to me, Eleanor, it's your husband who I'm concerned with, and you *must* know by now that his first and *only* love is for me!"

Tilly felt like laughing in her face, but judging by Rayne's statement, and the countless letters which she'd sent to August, she knew that this was an unhinged young woman who stood before her and was capable of anything. She sat silently, deciding to listen to everything Rayne had to say before making any kind of verbal protest.

Rayne hurried to the chest of drawers and returned proudly waving a silver bracelet in front of Tilly's face.

*"Look! Read this!* This is the very bracelet that August gave me when he pledged his undying love for me! It's the one I told you about in my letter, so don't think for a single minute that I was lying to you! August Miller loves *me* but now you have done exactly what your bloody mother did to our poor Pappa and ensnared him with an unwanted child. A burden to keep his heart in misery forever! Well, *Eleanor,* that is why I have done this and you might thank me one day; if you live to tell the tale, that is!"

She returned the bracelet to its drawer.

"Could I have some more water?" asked Tilly.

*"Is that all you have to say!"* cried Rayne, in anger.

"I will have more to say later, I'm sure, but my throat is dry and painful!"

"You don't look as though you're carrying a baby!" Rayne randomly announced as she refilled the glass.

Tilly lowered her eyes, not wanting to make eye contact with Rayne as her thoughts ticked over like an overwound clock. This might be her only chance at making a change to her outcome, but she didn't know Rayne well enough to predict how far she was prepared to go to reach her evil goals. Would being with child make any difference, she mused; if she was to be held captive for a long period it would be impossible to keep up the pretence of having a baby growing in her belly. Her decision was made and she looked up at Rayne, with the saddest of eyes.

"I lost my baby a week ago," she said in a quivering voice. "It was heartbreaking."

Rayne was silent but inside she felt a warmth and knew that this would make her plan far easier. She fed Tilly with the glass of water, but in light of the new revelation, her mind was now engrossed in concocting a new scheme.

# CHAPTER FIFTEEN

"Where do you think Tilly is, Mrs Ellie...do you think she might be dead?"

"*Charles!* How could you even think such thoughts? And it's *Miss Tilly* unless you wish me to inform your parents about your lack of manners," cried Eleanor, who had been permanently on the brink of tears since Tilly's disappearance four weeks ago. "Just for saying such a terrible thing, there will be no piano lesson today as well!"

"I'm sorry, Mrs Ellie! But I heard Mamma and Pappa talking this morning, and that's what they both think. Mamma said that if she was alive she would have written to us by now and that we would have heard something!"

"*Charles Hyde!* You are becoming a very discourteous young man! Listening in on a grown up's conversation!" Eleanor shook her head in disappointment as Charles turned red and chewed on his bottom lip.

"I expect every question on that paper to be answered by the time I return, Charles, and I don't want to see one mistake. *Do you understand?*"

"Yes Mrs Ellie," he replied grumpily.

"Oh Rosa, *what a morning!*" she declared, as she entered the kitchen where Rosa was busy baking. "Does *everyone* think that Tilly is dead?" Shocked by the question, Rosa immediately ceased rolling out the pastry and wiped her messy hands.

"Ellie! What's brought such thoughts to your head? Of course, I don't think she's dead. It's a mystery that's for sure, but most mysteries eventually get solved, don't they?"

"Apparently, those are the thoughts of Mr and Mrs Hyde! Charles has just informed me!" With a supporting arm around Eleanor, Rosa sighed heavily, "Oh, Ellie, you know how folk talk, and I expect that, as usual, Charles has muddled everything that he overheard and spoken completely out of turn; anyway, that young scallywag shouldn't have been listening in the first place! *Nosey parker!*"

"That's exactly what I said to him!"

"Let's have an early tea break before Felicity wakes from her morning nap. Oh, I do miss Tilly so much and have come to realise how much work she did about the place too. I pray every day that she will return to us soon."

"Me too, Rosa. I find myself thinking more about Tilly than of the baby, and the thought of Tilly not being around when my time comes breaks my heart!"

Rosa viewed Eleanor sympathetically, as she remembered all that she and Tilly had gone through together, knowing how strong their sisterly bond was. "Maybe, Mr Kelly will make a breakthrough soon."

"Noah Kelly must be the oldest and slowest private detective in England, Rosa! I think my August would find more leads than him! I've never come across such a slow-paced man before and as for the hundreds of cases he claims to have solved...well I find that impossible to believe! Where did Mr Hyde find him? He should have been put out to pasture years ago!"

"Ooh, dear, I can see that poor old, Noah Kelly is not your favourite person! I thought he was very thorough in his questioning, though!"

"Yes, he certainly was, but it takes more than questions to find a missing person! I'd like to know if he's actually been anywhere other than in his office, with his notebook under his nose. Didn't he mention how he detested the cold winds of March and the intermittent heavy downfall during April?"

Rosa couldn't help but giggle at Eleanor as she poured the boiling water into the teapot.

"I expect he'll not leave his office until mid-summer!" concluded Eleanor, crossly.

"Perhaps he dislikes the heat too!" added Rosa.

"Honestly, Rosa, if I wasn't carrying this baby and feeling so emotional, I'd be out on the streets conducting my own search for Tilly and I dare say, I'd make a better job of it than, *Mr Noah Kelly!*"

"You just wipe any such thoughts from your head, Ellie! Just remember I'm like your older sister and I mean what I say!"

"Well, you're beginning to sound more like my grandmother and August's mother!"

By the time Eleanor had calmed down over two cups of tea and some of Rosa's freshly baked, butter biscuits, August had returned from his morning at Hyde&Son. Working in the gentleman's shop was a far cry from what he'd rather be doing but it was the only way to make ends meet until his income from being an author increased substantially. His ambition was to write a complete series of detective novels, which would become best sellers. He greeted Eleanor in his usual loving way, the look of devotion as clear upon his face as it had been since their early days together. Rosa tactfully went into the back parlour where Charles had been as quiet as a mouse after upsetting Eleanor, earlier. He wanted to present her with perfect results when she returned, without a single error on the history paper.

"Is Mr Miller home, Rosa?" he inquired, politely.

"Yes young man, he is!"

His worried look didn't go unnoticed by Rosa.

"Is Mrs Ellie telling him what I said, Rosa?"

"Well, I wouldn't know, because I never listen into private conversations. But you did upset poor, Mrs Ellie this morning, Charles, so you'd better behave yourself in future, especially on sensitive subjects like Miss Tilly!"

As much as Charles felt the sudden urge to run

into Rosa's arms; whenever August was around, he was inclined to put on a brave face, not wishing August to consider him anything other than a young man.

Eleanor and August were soon in the parlour and August suggested that he and Charles should have a quick ball game in the garden, while Eleanor marked his work. Charles proudly handed her the paper,

"I'm sorry, Mrs Ellie, I didn't mean to upset you earlier. Please don't tell Mamma or Pappa!"

Eleanor smiled warmly, she adored Charles and could never find it in her to be cross with him for longer than a few minutes. She ruffled his soft curly hair and hugged him close.

"I think I answered every question correctly, Mrs Ellie!" he quickly added, before running off to the garden.

Later that afternoon, when Rosa had taken Charles and Felicity next door, leaving August to write and Eleanor to take her, now customary, afternoon nap, August announced that he too was disheartened by Noah Kelly's lack of success.

"Don't think me foolish, Ellie, but since I've been writing detective novels, I feel as though I'm beginning to think like a detective. You see, my darling, it's usually a case of elimination, followed by finding the common denominator after all the investigations have been completed!"

"Well, I must say, dearest husband, you even sound more proficient than Mr Kelly!" teased Eleanor.

"I'm serious, my darling, I've been thinking a lot into this puzzle and I'm almost one hundred per cent sure that your *delightful* half-sister is behind it!"

"Those were my initial thoughts too, but it's been a month now since she disappeared and I would have thought that Rayne Jackson would have been in touch by now, and what can she possibly gain by kidnapping Tilly?"

"I believe that she is waiting for either you or me to go in search of her!"

"It doesn't make sense, August! Why would Rayne even presume us to think she was behind her disappearance?"

August sighed heavily as he gently ran his hand across, Eleanor's slightly protruding belly, "I must do something, my sweetheart because I know that if Tilly isn't found, our baby will suffer; you've lost your beautiful smile my darling and this should be one of the happiest times of our lives together! Now, I must let you sleep while I don my detective's hat and write out my plan! "

"I'm sorry, August, but I can't help feeling that wherever Tilly is, she is being held against her will...or worse! She would never just go off like that and I'm certain she has no secrets from me too!"

"My darling, please don't cry...don't contemplate the worst...*please*...you'll only distress yourself further!"

As he cradled her in his arms, his mind trying desperately to tie each loose string together, by the time Eleanor had dozed off, August had made up his mind that he would board the London bound train first thing in the morning and call on Peggy.

*************

After meticulously sifting through the music hall's accounts, and questioning Tommy on his recent rendezvous with Sid Crewe, Buster could find nothing untoward going on. He had kept a close eye on Tommy since that day, who had not ventured to the Salty Dog inn again or had any additional secret meetings with Sid. Tommy had disclosed how he had merely been passing on an address to Sid and had been paid handsomely by one of the sailors who frequented the music hall. After warning him to stay clear of Sid Crewe and his associates, Buster was quite sure that the entire business was simply down to Tommy's lack of foresight and his habit of acting on impulse. Everyone and everything was ticking along smoothly in the music hall and the new and popular entertainment venue was already lining Buster's pockets, pleasing him even more that together, with Peggy's grocery, they were his only legitimate businesses and made for an excellent cover for his, not so above-board dealings. His initial intended revenge upon Edward Jackson via his daughter had now simmered down and although he was reminded of the awful period in his life every time he allowed himself to remember who Rayne's father was, deep in his heart he knew it would solve nothing if he turned on the young lass; she was providing a cover for him, earning him some pin money and most of all, she was keeping Tommy Kettle content and focussed on his job.

As every hour and day merged into another and with there being no way for Tilly to tell if it was night or day being locked away in the depths of the music hall, she felt as though she'd been Rayne Jackson's captive for months.

Intermittently nodding off to sleep in between long wakeful periods of complete boredom where the constant view of the four walls of the dressing room was sending her crazy, Tilly was sure that Ellie would have given birth by now. Her frustration had reached its pinnacle and she was also sure that Rayne had no plan for her and if she did, it had somehow gone wrong. She continuously wondered whether Eleanor and everyone in Paradise Street had any clue as to where she was and if they were out searching for her. She continued to harbour a strong sense that they were, if only to keep her spirits up, which was the only light illuminating her present dim world. She missed Felicity so much and hoped the sweet infant wouldn't forget her. She missed everyone and yearned so much to be set free. The occasional visit from the tall man who sneaked in from time to time bringing her food and drink became a treat which, as days went by, she quite looked forward to. He said his name was Tommy and he seemed to know quite a lot about the business of August and Eleanor. He had mentioned that he'd met August on a couple of occasions, expressing how sorry he was that it hadn't worked out between them and that August had married another. He claimed how, he too, had experienced such rejection in his life before. Although Tilly said little she sensed that she could easily coax Tommy into saying more. She listened with intrigue and the more she heard the more she came to realise that she was surrounded by a tangle of lies, and she'd have to be extra careful of saying anything which might cause them to realise that she wasn't Eleanor. By how he spoke of Rayne, Tilly knew that he was in love with her and as he begged her to accept Rayne as a proper sister so that she could be free of her shackles, Tilly instantly realised that Rayne was leading him along an evil path of deception and false hope. She toyed with the notion of speaking out to Tommy, but since he appeared to be blinded by his love for Rayne, he'd likely not believe a word of what she said. Tilly now knew that she was in the heart of Whitechapel and after listening to August's accounts of the area, knew that she was surrounded by a multitude of dangerous and unscrupulous men and women and had to be on her guard.

# CHAPTER SIXTEEN

Even though Peggy was absorbed in the running
of her new grocery and enjoying every minute of
it, the short-tempered and distant minded
behaviour of Rayne had not gone undetected to
her. Peggy worried that perhaps Buster Forbes
was putting too much pressure on her to work
longer hours and that Rayne was becoming
exhausted. She quite often arrived home late
these days or returned to the music hall after
supper, saying she had to practice some new
tunes in order to keep her audience satisfied.
Peggy decided to have words with Buster when
he next called on her and in the meantime keep a
watchful eye on her granddaughter.
With the country being overwhelmed by an
unusual blast of May heat, the dressing room
had become like a stifling oven. Rayne was
becoming impatient with the situation and so far
her plan was not running as she'd anticipated.
She had yet to receive a reply to the letter she'd
sent to August almost three weeks ago which
she hoped would be the first in a new weekly
correspondence with him until he overcame the
fact that his wife had walked out on him. She
doubted it would take him long, still convinced
that there couldn't possibly be any genuine love
shared by him and her half-sister, who she was
growing to despise more than ever. Since the

major obstruction to her future happiness was still taking up her dressing room there was only one option left. Eleanor would have to go. With her thoughts so deeply engrossed in her scheme, she paid little attention to Peggy's breakfast chit chat and walked to Commercial Street in a state of preoccupation. Tommy welcomed her as she drifted into the music hall, his smile wider than usual in the hope of gaining a little attention from Rayne.

"Let me take yer to that chop'ouse again after work, Rayne. I don't feel as though I've seen yer since Eleanor's bin 'ear!"

Rayne stared hard at him, her mind still miles away, but knowing that she might need Tommy if she was to go ahead with her plan, she managed to hold her tongue from speaking her cold-hearted thoughts.

"Why don't yer set 'er free, Rayne, it seems ter me that she don't want nought ter do wiv yer. Maybe she was 'appy in Oxf'rd. Yer can't force someone ter love yer, Rayne. You an' me could go out fer supper every night then!" he concluded eagerly.

Rayne felt sickened by his suggestion, she loathed Tommy Kettle and detested having to be so sweet to him and despised seeing him every day of her life. It was then and there that she came to the spontaneous decision and realised that she needed no more time to dwell on her plan. The quicker she eliminated Eleanor from her life the quicker she could flee to Oxford and set about winning August Miller's heart.

"I don't think Eleanor will ever wish to be my real sister. It breaks my heart, you know and to be quite honest with you, Tommy, I'm becoming a bit scared of her and of what she might do to me, should I set her free; she's made some terrible threats and she *is* illegitimate, after all, and you know how evil those type tend to be!"

Tommy was shocked by her announcement, he had spoken with Eleanor on quite a few occasions and he liked her, she appeared to have a soft heart and a kind and gentle character.

"I don't reckon it makes no difference, half of the folk in Whitechapel are *illig...illegi...*Oh, *bugger*, I don't take ter yer fancy words, Rayne but they's bastards, that's what I'm tryin' ter say, and they are all as nice as pie! Why don't yer just send 'er back ter Oxf'rd an' be done wiv it? She don't look as though she's capable ov 'arming no one!"

"*Exactly Tommy!* You see! She is a manipulative mongrel who has cunningly managed to pull the wool over your eyes with her sweet, honey tongue!"

Feeling totally confused as he scratched his head, Tommy had a feeling that if he lived to be a hundred, he'd never understand women.

"You don't seem to realise how heartbreaking this is for me, Tommy!" she sobbed, dramatically. "After all that I've done for that ungrateful girl. I went out of my way to have her rescued from Oxford and I only ever wanted to have the love of a sister, since I feel so alone in this cruel world! Mother has abandoned me, Grandmamma doesn't have many years left and I have no siblings apart from *her*!"

"Ah, please don't upset yerself," pleaded Tommy, as he gingerly placed his arm on her shoulder. "You've got me! An' in the future there'll be our nippers...you'll make a great ma, Rayne...yer can teach our kids 'ow ter play the fiddle too...we'll be right well off!'

His words had an instant nauseating effect on Rayne, she couldn't think of a worse scenario than spending her life with Tommy Kettle and bearing his children; she felt like shoving him out of the music hall doors and running forever, but somehow she kept her composure and smiled meekly at him.

"Let's meet for supper Tommy, but not at the chophouse, I want to talk and it's always so noisy there!"

Feeling instantly delighted, Tommy assured her of how he'd come up with a discreet place by supper time and left Rayne to go to her dressing room.

"Don't you think it's about time we put an end to this ridiculous situation, Eleanor!" screamed Rayne, the second she entered her dressing room. Startled by her aggressive tone and having only just woken, Tilly blinked profusely.

Rayne lit the lantern and stood arms akimbo, looking down on Tilly.

"*I've* had enough, even if *you* haven't and if you value your worthless life then you'd better do exactly as I ask of you!"

Tilly swallowed hard; there seemed to have been a dramatic change in Rayne's personality overnight and so she decided the less she said the better.

Rayne continued, "I'm going to untie your hands, but I'm warning you now, if you so much as think that you can overpower me, you'll regret it. You will never get out of this place alive...It is fully guarded and I have informed everyone, including Tommy of the situation! *Have I made myself clear?*"

"You most certainly have, dear *half-sister!*"

"Please refrain from calling me that too, the very thought that we have a blood connection turns my stomach and puts my teeth on edge! I am going to let you write to that poor unfortunate husband of yours!" she continued, with a slight smile shadowing her determined face as she mentioned August. "You will be doing him the greatest of favours by setting him free to find his way into my arms. August and I were made for each other, Eleanor, just as my parents were made for each other until your brazen mother seduced my poor pappa and ruined his life forever! Well, that's *not* going to happen to August because I intend to rescue him and save him from your scheming plans! It was a blessing that you couldn't manage to carry his child, Eleanor, even *you* must realise that! He loves me and married you out of pure pity! No doubt we will endure a long and happy marriage and I will enrich his life by producing our delightful children, who of course will be talented and extremely artistic!"

As Tilly listened with hidden amusement, she came to realise that Rayne Jackson's unhealthy infatuation with August had left her unbalanced and Tilly knew how irrational such a character was capable of behaving. Rayne had certainly convinced herself that August loved her and it appeared that she was prepared to go to any lengths to claim him as her own. How glad she was that, so far, nobody had realised that she wasn't Eleanor; just knowing that her dearest friend was safe and that she was paying her back for all of her favours over the years, sent a gush of satisfaction through her.

As Rayne rummaged around, noisily, in her small cupboard, soon pulling out a large pair of scissors and a small box. Tilly watched with intrigue and fear.

"I'm going to temporarily cut the ropes on your hands, but I will be securing them again once you've carried out my instructions! You are going to write a letter to August and explain how you had to leave him...explain how, after you lost the baby, you came to realise how you no longer loved him...*no*...actually confess that you never loved him in the first place but merely wanted a husband to support you! Convince him that you've fallen in love with another and that you intend to spend the rest of your life in his arms."

As Tilly listened closely to Rayne's insane idea, she reminded herself that she had to think and react as Eleanor would if she was actually her. Eleanor would be heartbroken if she were forced to write such hurtful lies to August, but then she doubted August would believe her. This was, in fact, a golden opportunity and would undoubtedly lead a rescue party to her aid and clarify how Tilly had been mistaken for Ellie.

"And what if I refuse to write such dreadful lies to my dear husband? What will be my fate?"

Rayne had a way of immediately changing her pretty face into the most hideous and wicked-looking form; she squinted her eyes and pursed her lips; her nostrils flared and her pale complexion turned bright crimson.

"I don't think that you'd like to hear the answer to that, Eleanor, but let's just say that you might just find it impossible to utter another word!"

The ropes were cut and as Tilly rubbed her raw wrists and flexed her fingers, Rayne placed the small writing box into her lap.

"Make it convincing now, and don't try to sneak any hidden messages into it, because if I'm not satisfied with it you will simply have to compose another one!"

The sudden rapping upon the door caused them both to jump in alarm, it was followed by the voice of Tommy, declaring how there was a full audience upstairs waiting for Rayne to play her violin.

"Looks as though you'll be able to pour your heart out in private! But don't get any silly ideas, Eleanor, because I will be locking the door behind me and expect a perfectly penned letter on my return!"

# CHAPTER SEVENTEEN

Tommy had persuaded the proprietor of a nearby Turkish, coffee house to allow him and Rayne a secluded table for the evening, it had cost him free tickets to the music hall which elated the owner's hard-working wife so much that she also cooked them a modest meal in appreciation. Since it was mostly men who frequented the coffee houses, Mr Tiryaki had placed a table in the passageway between the kitchen and the back entrance, insisting that nobody would bother them there. Tommy wondered if tonight would be the right time to officially bend on one knee and propose in true gentlemanly style to his beloved Rayne.

She followed him through the narrow alleyway off Whitechapel Street, curious as to where he was leading her. It was perfect, a quiet, secluded place where she could disclose her plans to him. Mr Tiryaki had instructed his waiter to keep the couple's cups continuously topped up with his infamous Turkish coffee; reputed to be one of the finest in the East End. It was a new taste to Rayne, who found its heavy flavour too bitter. Not missing the observant eye of Mrs Tiryaki, who had been peeping through the gap in the doorway from time to time, she immediately issued orders for the coffee to be exchanged for a refreshing glass of sweet mint tea.

"How did you manage to stumble upon such a cosy and secluded place, Tommy? I must say, *I am most* impressed; I thought it was only the likes of Buster Forbes who was gifted with the power of persuasion around these parts!"

"Buster Forbes is only gifted with a thickly lined pocket, Rayne and money talks! Besides, as I'm always telling you, I'd do anything fer you, me darlin'."

"Well, I hope you've not been left penniless, Tommy, because you will need some funds to follow out the next part of my plan, which is what I so desperately wanted to talk to you about!"

Rayne smiled widely at Tommy, noticing his sudden loss of spirits; she knew what he was thinking, but no matter how humiliating she was finding the task of having to string him along like a lovesick puppy, she knew that if she wanted her new plan to work, it was paramount that she kept Tommy sweet and hopeful.

"Why the solemn face, Tommy Kettle!" she teased, stretching her arm out and lovingly stroking his face. It was enough, and as if by magic, an instant smile returned upon Tommy's face. "It won't take too long, and then we have the rest of the evening to enjoy each other's company! We could even take a stroll along the embankment, beneath the May moon!"

"I'd like that Rayne, I'd like the entire world ter see yer on me arm."

They ate hurriedly, a special meal consisting of fish and tomatoes, infused with exotic and pungent spices which both Rayne and Tommy had never before tasted.

"These Turkish folk certainly know how to turn a boring river bloater into an extra delicious meal!" expressed Rayne.

"Give me a good old pie an' mash any day!" moaned Tommy. "I don't reckon me belly is gonna take ter these weird spices an' me mouth feels right strange!"

As Rayne clandestinely thought how boring and unsophisticated Tommy was, she also wondered if Eleanor had composed her letter by now, feeling quite excited by the thought of reading it.

"Tommy, I want you to take a trip to Oxford tomorrow!" she blurted out. " I will make sure that everything in the music hall ticks along nicely; perhaps you could allow one of your most trusted ushers to man the doors for the day, but make sure he understands that I am in charge. If Buster should show his face, I'll come up with a feasible story; like your ma has been taken poorly and she was asking for you! How does that sound?"

Shocked by the sudden request for him to travel to Oxford and abandon his job for the day, Tommy couldn't even begin to imagine what crazy scheme Rayne was now plotting.

"I don't like spouting lies 'bout me ma, Rayne. It ain't good ter tempt fate like that! And what the 'ell d'yer want me ter go ter Oxf'rd for? I'll likely get lost! I ain't never bin away from the East End afore, I ain't one fer travelling, Rayne, yer should know that by now!"

Sighing heavily, Rayne sensed that she'd have a difficult undertaking on her hands in convincing Tommy to follow her instructions.

"Come along Tommy, let's leave this place and go for a stroll, maybe those unusual spices have turned you into a coward!"

Hurrying out of the coffee house with Tommy chasing behind was not the way Tommy had envisaged the evening's events. With only half an hour left before he'd have to return to the music hall, Rayne's spiteful mood had left him feeling quite glum. He wondered why she wanted him to go to Oxford.

"Wait up, Rayne, what's got inter yer?"

Rayne, who was already marching down Whitechapel Street turned around and erupted into sobs. Tommy was quick to be at her side and, as usual, foolish enough to fall right into her sly trap. She sobbed dramatically against his chest and he relished in every sweet moment that she was in his arms.

"Oh, Tommy, please forgive me for being so rude...I honestly don't know what's happening to me, but I can only conclude that my distress is totally due to my *beastly* half-sister! I don't know what to do anymore, Tommy. I wish I'd never had her brought to Whitechapel...all I ever wanted was the opportunity to be a kind and loving sister! She has made the most terrible threats, Tommy, and even if I release her, she has vowed to take revenge, and make my life a misery for as long as she spares it! I'm terrified of what she might do...She *is* illegitimate when all's said and done. She must take after her wicked mother...I wouldn't even be surprised if she had fed my poor pappa with poison to end his life. I doubt there was anything whatsoever wrong with his heart!"

Taking a step back, Tommy was distressed by Rayne's accusations. He found it hard to believe that the petite, quiet natured, girl in Rayne's dressing room was capable of such menace, but at the same time, he had been warned many a time by his sisters and his mother of how deceptive and manipulating women could be and that he should never trust a female until he properly knew her and knew everything about her. He'd always presumed they were merely trying to protect him from being trapped into a forced marriage, but perhaps there was an ounce of truth in their warnings, he mused.

"Is that tiny lass capable ov carrying out such threats, Rayne? She don't look the type ter me....reckon she's just scared and so she's trying ter scare you an' all!"

"*Oh, Tommy!*" yelled Rayne, forgetting how busy the street was, "what do you know? You haven't been the one to listen to her continuous threats! I tell you, Tommy, Eleanor Whitlock is not the girl you imagine her to be. I discovered that the hard way. She is not to be trusted Tommy and you mustn't believe a word that springs from her deceitful mouth. She *has* to go Tommy and the sooner the better!"

Tommy kept quiet, there were far too many people around, all with the potential of listening in and using the information they heard to their advantage. Blackmail was commonplace in Whitechapel and he didn't intend to take any chances. They arrived at a narrow passageway, the back entrance to the adjoining shops, which were closed for the night, leaving the dead-end peaceful and empty. Tugging her arm, he steered Rayne down the passageway. She trembled and for a split second feared that she'd pushed Tommy too far and he'd been overcome by the devil and the sudden urge to take advantage of her. As she voiced a small cry, Tommy shushed her and beneath the distorted moonlight, Rayne could just make out how vexed he appeared.

*"What is it, Tommy?* Why are you taking me down this *ghastly* alley?"

They had reached the towering wall at the far end of the passageway, there was a pile of stinking rubbish and Rayne instinctively knew that there would be hungry rats nesting inches away from her feet. She shuddered.

"You can't be shouting yer mouth off 'bout

gettin' rid ov someone in the middle ov Whitechapel, Rayne! Nearly everyone knows who you are! Yer just askin' fer trouble!"

Rayne immediately realised that, for once, Tommy was right. She hadn't thought and had been so intent on persuading Tommy of her story that she saw no danger in what she was saying.

"Where would I be without you, Tommy? You are such a dear. I'm really sorry, I didn't think, but thank you!"

"So what exactly d'yer mean by *them* words, *she 'as ter go?*" quizzed Tommy. "I 'ope yer don't mean ter kill yer *sister*, Rayne! Cos that's what it sounded like ter me an' ter any listening ears which might 'ave been wagging, back there!"

"*Don't be silly*, Tommy! I couldn't harm a fly...*no*, I have a plan which involves sending her on a trip across the seas...sort of like hidden treasure! Far away, where it would take her a lifetime to save up the return fare!"

Tommy swallowed hard, he could taste Mrs Tiryaki 's spicy meal in the back of his throat.

"So, if I can arrange yer plan, will that be the end, Rayne? Will yer say, *yes*, an' wed me after that, Rayne?"

"I will definitely consider it, sweet Tommy, but a girl does need a proper proposal in the right atmosphere and this stinking place is far from the romantic one I've always dreamt of!"

"You're right, I shouldn't 'ave said nought about

marriage. So why do I 'ave ter go ter Oxf'rd then? What's that all about?"

"I want you to deliver a letter by hand, my darling! You won't have to see or talk to *anyone*, simply deliver the letter through the letterbox!"

"Why don't yer just stick a bleedin' stamp on it like most folk would do?"

"Because, my sweet Tommy, I've had *far* too many letters go astray in the past, and this is an extremely important one!"

"Well, I can't go termorra, cos Forbes is comin' ter check the bleedin' books again...reckon 'e's keepin' a close eye on me an' Gawd 'elp us if 'e finds out 'bout yer sister! We'll both be out on our ears!"

"Don't be such a coward, Tommy, he's hardly likely to go down to my dressing room while I'm on stage fiddling my heart out, now is he? Very well, you can go the day after, and by the way, where does that awful man dwell?"

"Who?" quizzed Tommy, aghast, "yer don't mean the bleedin' *scavenger* do yer?"

"What's his real name?"

"He's called, Sid Crewe and yer ter stay well clear ov 'im...'e's a nasty cove an' 'e ain't called *the scavenger* fer no reason!"

"Oh, I saw that puny old man!" voiced Rayne, mockingly. "He doesn't scare me in the least; anyone can give themselves an intimidating title!"

"Just stay away from 'im, Rayne! *Understand!*"

roared Tommy, his face consumed with anger.

# CHAPTER EIGHTEEN

Rayne couldn't have been more satisfied with Tilly's letter; she'd written everything that she wanted her to say and was now, even more, certain that once it was in the hands of August, he'd realise how blinded he'd been by Eleanor's false love. Undoubtedly, he would be upset, she considered, but that would give her the perfect opportunity to strike and offer all the sympathy and affection she could muster and prove to him what an ideal match they would make. With the letter secure in her reticule and Eleanor, once again, bound and gagged, Rayne felt a spring in her step as she headed home knowing that this messy episode would soon be drawing to an end and before long, Eleanor would be out of her life forever, and the beginning of a remarkable romance with the handsome and talented, August Miller, would commence.

Shocked to discover that her grandmother had already closed the grocery for the evening, which was most odd, Rayne hurried across the threshold, praying that she wasn't about to be punished for her illicit actions and find her grandmother ill, or worse. Sat at the parlour table in a trance, Peggy was clutching a crumpled letter in her veiny hands. Rayne felt her heart drop, fearing it was from August and that he'd somehow discovered her part in

Eleanor's abduction.

"*Grandmamma!* Is something wrong?" she exclaimed, as she tried to view the writing on the scrunched up letter.

"I can't believe it, Rayne, I just can't believe it! How could I have delivered such a selfish hard-hearted woman into the world?"

With an immediate sense of relief, Rayne knew that the letter must be from her mother.

"Let me brew some tea, Grandma and then you can tell me all about it!"

"She's leaving *tomorrow*, you know and expects us to be at Euston station by six in the morning, to say goodbye to her...probably forever! I think she's completely forgotten her responsibilities and overlooked her duties as your mother and as my daughter! Utterly selfish is my Elizabeth! *Utterly selfish!*"

"Putting the tea on hold, Rayne joined her grandmother at the table. "Where on earth is she going, Grandma?"

"*India!* She's sailing from Liverpool to India tomorrow evening!"

"*India!*" repeated Rayne, in alarm.

"Her companion's sister passed away a few months ago, leaving behind a palace, by all accounts, complete with a household of servants and personal ayahs, not to mention a small fortune, so she wants to take your mother with her to reside there permanently! Of course, it's exactly the sort of lifestyle which your mother has been yearning for ever since your dear pappa left this world! No doubt she'll be in her element again surrounded by riches and servants!"

"*Grandmamma!* I can't, for the life of me, understand why you're finding this news so upsetting; we've barely seen her since she left Whitechapel, she might as well be in India, and besides, if I know Mamma, she will detest the heat and the wildlife out there! She couldn't even handle a polite London rat, who simply wanted some crumbs! How do think she will react to a snake or a giant cockroach, the size of a plate?"

"There's another reason she's going too, Rayne!" Rayne looked curiously at her grandmother, "What reason, Grandma?"

"She claims that she intends to find a suitable match for you out there from within the Queen's regiments. She writes how there are some of the most eligible, high ranking, young men who would make the perfect husband for you Rayne!"

"Well, she's very much mistaken there! I don't intend to set one foot on Indian soil and I certainly don't wish to spend my life married to a man of Mamma's choosing! How dare she think she can interfere in my life whenever it suits her and ignore me for the rest of the time! And I'm not traipsing across London before the sun rises to say my farewells neither! She should have come here to see us and to inform us of her intentions, not left it until the last minute, and upon the lines of a miserable letter!"

Peggy sniffled into her handkerchief paying little attention to Rayne's angry protest. "My only child has given me nothing but a life of misery, Rayne! Sometimes I feel so alone in the world that it breaks my heart!"

"You have me Grandmamma and you have your lovely grocery shop which you've dreamt of having all your life. You have hundreds of friends and well-wishers too! Do You know that I get stopped every few yards when I'm out, with folk asking after you! You are truly loved around here and I don't believe it's true what they say about blood being thicker than water! Just take my so-called *half-sister*; she isn't bothered with me in the least!"

Peggy was quick in her defence, "Now, that's not fair, Rayne, Eleanor is expecting her first baby and I doubt that young Mr Miller would allow her to travel to London even if she had her heart set on it. I'm quite sure you will meet each other one day and when it comes to dear Eleanor, blood certainly isn't thicker than water...I do believe I love that lass almost as much as I love you!"

Feeling a surge of jealousy rushing through her veins, Rayne had to bite her tongue in order not to speak out. How could her grandmother possible love that girl who was sat in her dressing room, she wasn't even as pretty as she'd claimed her to be neither? No, mused Rayne, there was certainly nothing at all special about Eleanor Whitlock, in appearance or personality.

"Why don't you go and see Mamma off in the morning, you can make an excuse for me; tell her I'm suffering from my monthly stomach cramps and unable to leave my bed!"

"Rayne!" admonished her grandmother, "I couldn't possibly mention such a matter in public!"

"Well make *any* excuse for me, Grandmamma, because wild horses couldn't drag me to Euston station in the morning!"

With the atmosphere suddenly turning icy, Rayne set about making the tea, with thoughts of her plot still uppermost in her mind. She would not allow her mother's flighty actions to ruin her plans, she mused.

With the promise that she'd clean the windows of the grocery, both inside and out, while Peggy journeyed to Euston station, Peggy left Whitechapel with Rayne's, hurriedly written, letter of well wishes to her mother. There was nothing Peggy could say to persuade Rayne to accompany her, but she could understand how hurt and rejected a young girl would feel in such circumstances.

As the sleeping sun began to push her way through the murky blue sky, Rayne set to work with her pail of water, deciding to work from the outside in, before Whitechapel Street became alive with folk. Little time has elapsed before the familiar, scrawny figure of Sid Crewe, skulking his way towards her couldn't have been a more welcoming sight.

'I'll teach Tommy a thing or two,' she thought, 'I'll show him just how tough a lass can be!'

"Mr Crewe!" she uttered as he neared her, his head bowed down as though he were looking for treasure upon the street. He glanced up, his face displaying its usual weathered and exceedingly angry expression.

 "Do you have time to talk, Mr Crewe, only I have a small favour I'd like from you, call it a business proposition, Mr Crewe."

Sid Crewe looked stealthily over his shoulder, "Some bleedin' cove is out ter skin me alive, so if yer lets me inside yer shop, you'll be doing me a great favour, an' we might just 'ave a deal!"

Rayne liked what she was hearing, it meant that she already had the upper hand on the notorious man they called the scavenger. She was quite assured that Sid would be willing to support her plan. Hoping that, at such an early hour, the neighbours wouldn't be watching, she quickly invited Sid over the threshold and led him through to the parlour. His beady eyes surveyed every square inch of the grocery shop as he tried to conceal his smug grin from Rayne.

 "You're quite safe now, Mr Crewe, nobody will find you here, and my Grandmamma won't be returning for hours!"

It was music to Sid's grimy ears, he couldn't believe how naive and foolish the fiddle girl was. She had obviously underestimated his notorious reputation, he mused.

"Yer best stop callin' me *Mister Crewe*, I ain't no bleedin' toff, Miss! Call me Sid!"

"Would you like some refreshments, *Sid?*"

"Well, I doubt yer keep the kind of refreshment whats I 'ave in mind, so a cup of Rosie Lee will see me right, I s'pose!"

"If you mean *whiskey*, Mr...I mean, Sid, well you'd be wrong there. My grandma keeps it hidden beneath the counter. The kindly, Mr Forbes keeps her well supplied, especially since he's quite partial to a drop when he pays us a call."

"D'yer mean *Buster Forbes?*" asked Sid, trying not to sound as thrilled as he felt.

"Of course, I do. He owns this shop, you see!"

"Is that a fact? Well, terday is turnin' out ter be full of surprises!"

"So, Sid, should I fetch you a glass of whiskey, then?"

"Nah, reckon I needs ter keep a clear 'ead if I'm gonna listen ter the job yer 'as fer me. Go make us a good ol' brew, *Miss fiddle girl,* an' a toasted muffin would be a right treat an all!"

"Well, you make yourself at home, Sid, I'll just be in the kitchen!"

Sid sniggered merrily to himself, "stupid little

upstart!" he muttered under his breath, nobody "ain't got a bleedin' kitchen 'round these parts. I'll bloody well teach 'er an' that bleedin' bastard, Forbes a lesson, one which won't be forgotten in an 'urry!"

With one eye on the scullery door, Sid made a hasty dash into the shop, his focus shifting in every direction. It took less than a few seconds for him to find what he was looking for; a spare key to the front door. He hurriedly tested it out before shoving it deep into his pocket and returning to sit at the table like a well-mannered guest.

Devouring the toasted muffin as though he'd not eaten for a week, Rayne was repulsed by his sloppy manners. She diverted her eyes, not wishing to witness the food being churned around in Sid Crewe's gaping mouth. He wiped his greasy face on the sleeve of his, already, heavily stained jacket sleeve before slurping his tea. The sweet-smelling parlour was soon overcome by his obnoxious body odour and whilst Rayne sipped, elegantly, from her cup, she realised she'd have to expel Sid Crewe out of her home as soon as possible, to give her time to air the place before her grandma's return. Thankfully, it seemed that Sid was also in a hurry to leave, so with the plan quickly discussed and with Sid boasting how he was capable of any job offered to him, he surprised Rayne by asking for payment in way of a bottle of whiskey. Praying that it would be a while before her grandmother noticed she was a bottle short, Rayne was sure that it was Sid Crewe's appreciation of her saving him from whoever he was running from, which had made for a bargain deal.

By the time Peggy returned home, the windows were sparkling clean, and the pleasant aroma of beeswax polish reached every corner of the modest parlour. Feeling proud of her achievements, Rayne hurried off to work in high spirits, vowing to keep her morning's events a secret from Tommy, until her plan had been completed successfully.

# CHAPTER NINETEEN

"Are you quite certain there's nothing wrong, Doctor Thompson?" pleaded August, overcome with anxiety.

"My dear young man, I assure you that the odd twinge and stomach cramp can be quite common in Eleanor's condition, especially since she underwent stomach surgery not so long ago. You are not to worry and by that, I mean both of you! But I do insist that Eleanor has complete bed rest for the next two days, at least!"

"I'm sorry to have dragged you across Oxford, Doctor Thompson, but I find it so difficult to trust any other doctor; you've been my physician throughout my entire life!"

Doctor Thompson smiled warmly at Eleanor, fondly remembering dear, Beatrice which left him with a heavy ache in his chest. He doubted there would ever come a day when Eleanor didn't stir those feelings of passion within him whenever he faced her; she was uncannily the image of Beatrice Whitlock.

"I'm here whenever you need me, Mrs Miller and don't you ever forget that," assured Albert Thompson. "Now, what's this I hear about poor young Tilly going missing? Doesn't sound like the Tilly we know, at all!"

"Exactly, Doctor Thompson!" exclaimed Eleanor. "We are all completely out of our minds with worry!"

"I was intending to take a trip to Whitechapel today, Doctor Thompson, but that was before Eleanor felt unwell!"

Doctor Thompson continued to look down, concernedly at Eleanor who was now sat up on her bed, with a little more colour returned to her cheeks.

"It's no wonder that you're suffering from stomach cramps, young lady! Too much worry for any young woman to be burdened with, let alone one who is with child!"

"I can't help worrying, Doctor Thompson; it's human nature, and I love Tilly as though she were my sister. I feel so *utterly* helpless!"

"I don't think it at all wise for you to travel while Eleanor is not feeling her best, August!" he stressed, turning his whole body to face August. "She needs you by her side, and with all due respect, it would be like looking for a needle in a haystack. I've been to Whitechapel, you might recall, in my attempt to find our most treasured, Eleanor!"

"And so have I, Doctor Thompson, but there's no need to worry because I will definitely not be going now. My first and paramount duty is to take care of my darling wife!"

"Good man, I'm glad you've seen sense, besides, young Tilly could be anywhere. On what basis are you searching in Whitechapel?"

"Because that's where my horrid half-sister lives

and it would appear that she is madly in love with August!" cried Eleanor, in distress.

With raised eyebrows, Doctor Thompson, tilted his head, waiting for a further explanation.

"She is positively infatuated with him Doctor and I fear she would stoop to any trick in the book in her aim to gain his affections! She is using Tilly as bait to catch her fish!"

"With August being that *very fish!*" said Doctor Thompson, intrigued by what he was hearing

"It's a serious matter, Doctor Thompson!" added August. "I received an abundance of correspondence from her which she'd mailed to East Hanwell, and in every one of them she pledged her undying love for me!"

"And my *only* letter simply informed me that August loved her with a passion and that I was to set him free from my evil trap! She compared me to my dear mamma, and how she believed she trapped my pappa in the same way!"

Doctor Thompson was instantly reminded of his own obsession with Beatrice Jackson, he knew that if he'd been an unattached and younger man and not a respected pillar of the community, he might have behaved quite foolhardy to gain his way into the arms and life of Beatrice, but then he doubted she would have been so flirtatious with him, should he have been in such a humble position. If anyone in the world knew how it felt to yearn for the arms of someone out of your reach, it was him.

"She's absolutely mad!" declared Eleanor, breaking into Doctor Thompson's distant thoughts.

"Young and foolish, maybe, but I don't think she's ready to be admitted to the lunatic's asylum quite so soon! It is my opinion that she hasn't yet recovered from the loss of her father. Grief can affect people in many ways and forms, but in my recollection of the young Miss Rayne, from my brief time spent in her company, I don't think she is a threat and she's certainly not capable of kidnap. No, a few harmless letters from a love-struck girl, jealous maybe that her half-sister has the love and devotion of a handsome young man while she feels alone in the world!"

"Well at least she still has her mother, and her grandmother, Peggy!" voiced Eleanor, crossly.

"Doctor's orders were that you relax and remain calm!" admonished Doctor Thompson, issuing Eleanor with a stern glare.

August was quick to take hold of Eleanor's hand, repeating the Doctors instructions to her in a softer tone.

Since Tilly's mysterious disappearance, Prudence and Winifred now spent more time sat in the front parlour, where they had a full view of Paradise Street. Immediately recognising Doctor Thompson, even though they'd only met once before, at Eleanor's and August's wedding, they prayed that his call was merely a social one, and not wanting to appear too meddlesome, waited anxiously for him to return to his gig. As August escorted Doctor Thompson out of the house, the two women were waiting outside with a string of questions.

"Ma! Grandma Prudence!" uttered August, a little surprised to find them on the doorstep.

"We were just about to call on young Ellie!" they declared in unison. "And then we caught sight of the good doctor alighting from his vehicle!" added Winifred.

"Nothing to worry yourselves with Ladies! I assure you, Eleanor is in the best of health but just in need of a little bed rest!"

With their sense of relief immediately apparent, they suggested how they'd be delighted to take care of Charles and Felicity for the day, which would enable Eleanor to have some peace and quiet and Rosa could get on with her household chores without being continuously disturbed. August liked the idea and accepted without further ado; it would also allow him to put pen to paper and work on his book, he considered.

************

Feeling as though he'd set foot into another world, Tommy felt completely out of place as he marched through the thoroughfares of Oxford. Glad that he'd worn his smart work suit for the journey, his gangly figure towered above everyone and he sensed that folk were furtively eying him. Did they know he was a stranger he thought; he certainly felt awkward and was already missing the familiar overcrowded and run-down streets of Whitechapel. Knowing that he'd have to ask someone for directions to Paradise Street, he warned himself that if he didn't pluck up courage to ask someone quickly, he'd most likely be walking in circles all day long and miss the return train. Nothing could be worse than having to spend a night in this strange and somewhat unfriendly looking City, he mused as he stepped warily over the threshold into a small and empty tobacconist's shop.

"Good afternoon, Sir!" greeted the shopkeeper enthusiastically, "and what a delightful afternoon it is too!"

Tommy nodded his head in reply, as he viewed the well-stocked shop. He had no intention of making a purchase and was already regretting entering such an expensive shop, merely for information.

"D'yer 'appen ter know where Paradise Street is, Gov?" he blurted out, rather coarsely.

The shopkeeper was visibly astonished by Tommy's rough and unusual accent, immediately viewing him as a threat.

"Would Sir care to purchase anything this afternoon?" he asked, timidly.

"Nah, Gov like I said, I need ter get ter, Paradise

Street an' deliver a message afore I miss me bleedin' ride 'ome!"

The shopkeeper didn't consider himself a coward and credited himself on being able to negotiate his way out of most heated situations, but that was amongst the locals. Immediately feeling threatened by the offensively speaking stranger, he felt the beads of sweat surface his brow.

"Indeed, it would be my pleasure to give Sir directions!" he voiced in a shaky voice.

The tobacconist peered through the shop window watching the gangly stranger march along the High Street. He wondered what business such a person would have with any of the residents of Paradise Street as it suddenly dawned on him how the reputable, Mr and Mrs Hyde lived in that very street. He wondered if he should call in at Hyde&Son to inform them, but as a flurry of customers came into his shop he decided that he'd simply mention it when he next encountered them, after all, he mused, the man had said how he simply wanted to deliver a letter.

\*\*\*\*\*\*\*\*\*\*\*\*

Following the visit from Doctor Thompson, the morning had proved relatively productive for August, and now, with Eleanor taking her afternoon nap and seeming far more relaxed since August had cancelled his journey to

Whitechapel, he decided to join his mother and grandma Prudence to ensure that Charles and Felicity weren't over exhausting them. He quickly swallowed the last mouthful of strong, tepid coffee and stepped out onto the bright street. As the sun's strong rays caused him to squint, it was a second later that he suddenly became aware of a casting shadow. Instantly glancing up at Tommy Kettle's lofty figure, for a moment in time he thought his troubled mind was playing tricks on his eyes. He continued to stare; he knew this man but somehow he looked out of place as he stood before him. Tommy stared hard at August, feeling less hostile towards him now knowing how his darling Rayne no longer held a torch for the handsome author. There was a moment of awkwardness as the two men were both lost for words. Tommy wondered if he should speak or merely place the letter into August Miller's hands and rush off, but in his slowness to make a decision, it was August who broke the uncomfortable standoff.

 *"Tommy Kettle!"* he quizzed, with a wrinkled brow.

"Gotta letter for yer, Mister Miller!"

"A letter?" repeated August, sounding confused. "What brings you to this part of the world, Tommy?"

"It's this bleedin' letter, ain't it! Rayne don't trust the Queen's mail ter deliver it safely! So she asked me ter deliver it meself."

Nothing about TommyKettle had changed, thought August, Tommy was still at the beck and call of that spoilt girl, but this surprising incident was indeed a miracle in itself, and August felt as though Whitechapel had come to him and he didn't intend to let Tommy leave in a hurry without a thorough but polite interrogation.

"Well, I can only presume that it must be a letter of the utmost importance!" stated August, thinking that perhaps Rayne was eager to make amends with her half-sister, at last, and had turned over a new leaf. "You must come in, Tommy and refresh yourself before returning! It is certainly a lengthy distance to have travelled just to deliver a letter!"

Feeling both hungry and thirsty, Tommy couldn't resist the offer, even if Rayne's warning words, that he should talk to nobody in Paradise Street, were bouncing around inside of his head. But, he considered, she need never know and as he'd often heard his mother say, what the eye didn't see, the heart didn't grieve over.

# CHAPTER TWENTY

August shared a wary glance with Rosa as he introduced Tommy, telling her that he was from Whitechapel and a close friend of Eleanor's half-sister. In a slightly nervous voice, Rosa declared how she would bring them a tray of refreshments to the front parlour, sensing that perhaps the towering man might know something of Tilly's whereabouts.

"Take a seat, Tommy, you must be weary from your travels!"

Tommy obeyed, immediately sitting in one of the winged armchairs, which appeared far too small for his lanky frame.

"I was right sorry ter 'ear 'bout you an' Miss Eleanor!" he professed. "But I reckons yer new bride must be right beautiful!"

It felt as though Tommy was talking in riddles as August listened in confusion.

*"My new bride?"*

"What's 'er name? Don't reckon Rayne told me."

"How is Rayne, is she in good health?"

"Ah, Rayne is me, true love, Mister Miller, she's me 'ole world an' I reckons it won't be long 'til we'll be askin' yer good self ter come ter our very own weddin'!"

August immediately felt sorry for Tommy and was reminded of the nasty and disrespectful way in which Rayne had referred to him during their encounter. Tommy was, sadly, blinded by his love for Rayne and by all accounts, it seemed that she was still taking full advantage of that fact. As Rosa arrived with a tray of tea and sandwiches, August opened the letter and before he'd reached the second line he realised that it had been penned by Tilly. He felt a deep and disturbing shadow draw over him; up until this moment, he'd underestimated how wicked Rayne Jackson could be. She was clearly a young woman with a distorted mind. Poor, brave Tilly, he mused, she was, without doubt, a loyal sister to Eleanor.

Tommy munched hungrily on the sandwiches, oblivious to the strain etched upon his host's face.

"If you'll excuse me for a moment, Tommy, I'll be back shortly."

"Hmmm," was all Tommy could voice with his mouth stuffed full.

Happy that Eleanor was still fast asleep, August crept stealthily across the room and retrieved the pile of letters. He intended to shock Tommy once and for all with the hurtful truth about his so-called future bride and hurriedly returned to the parlour where Tommy had managed to devour the entire platter of sandwiches, in his short absence.

"Here, Tommy, I'd like you to read these!"

Tommy's eyes lit up as though he'd been given a special treat, "*Letters? Fer me?*"

"Just read them if you would, Tommy."

He was a slow and poor reader, appearing to stumble over many of the words, but as August sat fully focussed on him it was soon apparent by Tommy's changing expression that he was beginning to see a clear picture.

"Read these out ter me, Mister Miller; I was always better wiv me numbers than me letters and Rayne pens some right posh words which I can't get ter grips wiv!"

August did as requested and had only reached the third letter when Tommy had finally heard enough, realising how he was still being strung along by Rayne.

"That's more than me ears can take, Mister Miller! Yer must think me a right old Charlie! That bleedin' bint 'as got me under 'er evil spell again, but this time there ain't no going back...I'm done wiv, bleedin' *Rayne Jackson!*"

August sat quietly, while Tommy came to grips with the shocking truth. He sympathised with this kind-hearted soul, whose love for Rayne had caused him nothing but humiliation and torment.

"That's it, Mister Miller, I'm gonna return ter Whitechapel an' bring Miss Eleanor back to yer first thing ter morro' morning, and then I'm gonna get meself as far away from that two-faced jezebel as soon as possible, even if it means 'aving ter quit the best job I've ever 'ad!"

August could detect Tommy's unshed tears as he

viewed his bright crimson face; he realised that, perhaps, Rayne was far more dangerous and a bigger threat to him and Eleanor than he'd initially suspected. It seemed that she was prepared to stretch to any lengths and hurt whoever stood in her way, in a bid, to try and gain his love.

"*Tommy!* My wife is upstairs sleeping! I believe that the poor soul you are holding prisoner is Miss Tilly! She works and lives here in this very house and is also like a *dear sister* to Eleanor!"

Tommy's jaw dropped and his mouth remained open as he stared in horror at August.

"*Sleeping?*" he, at last, muttered, looking even more confused.

"She is with child, Tommy and often sleeps during the afternoon!"

"But I thought...Oh, bleedin' 'eck...she's spouted me lie after lie...she must be laughing 'er bleedin' bloomers off be'ind me back!"

"But don't you see, Tommy!" expressed August, eagerly, "Rayne's sly and wicked plan has completely backfired on her if she believes Tilly to be Eleanor!"

The parlour door opened slowly and Eleanor popped her head into the room, curious as to who their visitor was.

"Ellie, my darling!" welcomed August, as he jumped out of his seat to greet her. "Come and join us...this is Mr Tommy Kettle from Whitechapel!"

His name sounded immediately familiar to her, "Good afternoon, Mr Kettle," she said in a small voice, fearing that he had arrived with bad news about Tilly.

Tommy was once again rendered speechless as he gawped at Eleanor, dumbstruck by her beauty and her golden tresses. She was like an angel he considered, and she lit up the entire room with her presence.

"Sit down, my love, and read this letter which Tommy has, so kindly, hand-delivered!"

Her look of confusion soon vanished as she recognized the writing, "*This is Tilly's handwriting!*" she exclaimed, appearing a little flushed. August poured her a cup of tea as she read the letter. Suddenly everything became clear; she felt her heart expand with love for her dearest friend.

"*Darling, Tilly*! She has been pretending to be me for all this time! Where is she, Mr Kettle? *Please tell me that she is safe and well?*"

Tommy swallowed hard before addressing Eleanor, feeling quite bashful all of a sudden.

"She's tied up in the basement of Forbes Entertainment 'all, Miss! She be in Rayne's dressing room!"

"*Oh poor Tilly!*" gasped Eleanor, on the brink of tears.

"Don't upset yourself, my darling! This is turning out to be a marvellous day...and Tilly will soon be back here, where she belongs."

"I hope you've been treating her well!"
Feeling his face burning, the image of Tilly, tied, and for much of the time, gagged, filled Tommy's mind.

"I promise yer, Miss Eleanor, that the minute I set foot in that dressing room, I'm gonna untie 'er ropes!"

Eleanor took in a sharp breath, no longer able to curb her tears.

As the three of them sat discussing the best way of handling the fragile situation, time passed by unnoticed. Austin and Wilma Hyde soon returned from work, and the news of Tilly was once again repeated. Rosa in the meantime, whilst popping next door to bring Charles and Felicity home for dinner, informed Winifred and Prudence of the new developments. They were overjoyed by the news, as was young master Charles, who knew that his beloved, Mrs Ellie would soon be back to her cheerful old self again, just as soon as Miss Tilly returned.
Since Tommy had now missed the last train back to London it was decided that he would stay the night and he and August would embark on the freeing of Tilly first thing in the morning, riding on the early milk train if necessary.

*************

It came as a huge relief to Rayne that Tommy had still not returned from his journey to Oxford, she glanced at the huge wall clock in the foyer of the music hall before nervously peering down Commercial Street, praying that Sid Crewe was not about to let her down. Her thoughts seemed to jump from one concern to another as she wondered how her grandmother would take the news that she was going to move to Oxford. She hoped that Buster Forbes wouldn't take the loss of his fiddle girl out on her grandma by evicting her from the grocery shop. Surely he couldn't be that mean to an old woman, she consoled herself. The noisy rattle of a costermongers barrow soon brought her out of her reverie and in an instant, the appearance of Sid Crewe and his heavily built accomplice sent another wave of nervousness through her. She hoped with all her heart that she wasn't overstepping the mark with her cruel plan, as the image of Newgate prison along with the dreadful tales she'd heard about the place sprung to mind. But, she reflected, who would ever find out that she was behind it? After all, she was just the innocent young, *fiddle girl*.

Sid Crewe stepped over the threshold of the music hall, closely shadowed by his accomplice who was carrying a huge wooden crate in his arms.

"Where is she then?" he demanded, his beady eyes boring into Rayne. She suddenly realised how cold his eyes appeared, there was not the slightest hint of any emotion in them and Rayne sensed it to be the sign of a man with no soul and a callous heart. "Where's the bleedin' bint yer wants shifting, fer Gawd's sake!" he spluttered, impatiently. "We ain't got all night!"

"Oh, um, er, she's down in the basement!"

*"Well go an' fetch 'er then!"*

Rayne felt intimidated by the men's presence. The overbuilt man was void of any facial expression and stood like a cold stone statue, staring down at Rayne as though he might suddenly gobble her up in one mouthful.

"But what if she tries to escape?"

"Just bring 'er up 'ere an' leave the experts ter do the rest!" mocked Sid.

Tilly's eyes opened wide as she heard the key turn, she prayed it would be Tommy with some victuals for her. Starving and thirsty, she was sure she'd been forgotten about, but the instant she set eyes on Rayne, an immediate overwhelming sense that something was about to change sent an icy chill through her body. Rayne's demeanour was oddly different, and although managing to hide it behind her confident façade, Tilly could still detect her apprehension. She marched towards Tilly with her head held high, emphatically declaring how she was about to set her free, which in itself was a statement Tilly found unbelievable.

"I'm going to untie the ropes around your ankles, Eleanor so that you can climb the stairs!"

"How kind you are, my dear half-sister!" replied Tilly, sarcastically.

It was an impossible endeavour for Tilly to climb the stairs, her leg muscles had wasted away during the weeks she'd been held captive and she collapsed on the third step, leaving her terrified that after weeks of imprisonment, she'd end up falling to her death on the stone stairs.

*"What's wrong with you, Eleanor!"* yelled Rayne in distress, "Now is not the time to be playing silly games...you'll only live to regret it!"

*"It's not my fault!"* she cried out in distress. "I can't feel my legs anymore, you left me in that damned chair for too long!" Tilly's uncontrollable tears streamed down her pale and gaunt cheeks.

"Just sit down on the step, while I go and fetch help." Convinced that Tilly was not bluffing, Rayne felt assured that she wasn't capable of dashing to freedom.

A few minutes later Tilly recognised the heavily built man who had played a part in her abduction. She felt her insides contract and an immediate wave of nausea filled her mouth with foul-tasting bile. Her head began to spin and in a split second, as the chloroform soaked cloth came down upon her face, Tilly's thoughts came to an abrupt end. Hoisted over the man's shoulder like a butcher's carcass, she was carried up the stairs to the foyer. In an undignified manner, her body was quickly wrapped in a filthy blanket and thrust into the large wooden crate. Sid Crewe assisted in the nailing down of its lid before his accomplice hurled the crate onto the waiting barrow. The operation was completed in a few fleeting minutes leaving Rayne with an uncomfortable feeling of guilt and inwardly worried that her frail half-sister might not survive the journey ahead of her. The evening entertainers had begun to arrive in the music hall along with the flamboyantly painted ladies, who vulgarly flaunted their almost bare bosoms in precariously low cut gowns. Their cheap perfume sickened Rayne as she greeted them politely, all the while keeping a watchful eye out for the return of Tommy.

# CHAPTER TWENTY-ONE

Having seen better days, the antiquated, square-rigged clipper had once stood out like a beacon upon the high seas. Destined to be broken up after decades of seafaring, Felix Willow had succeeded in the winning bid for the worn-out sailing ship at auction, but instead of turning her into firewood, to sell on, he set about restoring her, not to her former glory, but just enough to render her seaworthy again. He foresaw the potential to venture into a money-making contraband run and soon became notorious around the East End as a fair and shrewd smuggler who had so far managed to outwit the official customs officers. Renamed *The Golden Moon*, she was dull in comparison to her glorified name, but Felix Willow had been confident that she was a clipper fit for any violent sea storm and would make him a wealthy man before he eventually hung up his sailing hat. Ten years on, he was still relishing in his new and adventurous lifestyle, declaring openly how he was now married to the sea, claiming how she would lure him back time after time and give him a taste of every possible mood, just as any wife would do. Admired and well known by every sailor and docker in the Pool of London, Felix was an unkempt but healthy-looking fifty-year-old who wore a permanent and radiant smile upon his weathered face, proud that he was one of the few men of his age with a full set of strong teeth. Felix was growing impatient; he was already late for his departure and had intended to pull up anchor over an hour ago. He had some business to settle up in Liverpool before setting sail to South America, but he owed Sid Crewe more than one favour and *the scavenger* wasn't a man who anyone wished to get on the wrong side of. 'Come on Crewe, what's keeping yer, fer 'heaven's sake?' he mumbled under his breath as he hung over portside scouring the docks. It was late and with the opaque moon hid behind thick rain clouds and only a dim glow radiating from a few of the ship's lanterns, every man on the docks became a moving shadow. The approaching squeak from the costermonger's barrow immediately told Felix that it was sure to be Sid Crewe; only he would wheel around such a disturbing cart.

"*Aye, aye Captain!*" called out Sid, mockingly.

"What's taken yer so bleedin' long, Crewe? I was planning ter dock in Liverpool by now!"

"Bin one ov them day's, me old friend, but I'll make it worth yer while, Willow; that I can promise yer. Send me down a couple of yer strongest mates will yer!"

Felix stared suspiciously at the large crate. "Yer never told me what it was that yer wanted shipping 'alf way 'cross the world, Crewe."

"Well yer in fer a surprise ain't yer, cos it's none uvver than one ov, Jackson's mongrel daughters!"

It took a lot to shock Felix Willow, but this news instantly made his jaw drop. "D'yer mean, *Edward Jackson?*"

"The very same!" voiced Sid, smugly. "Now are yer gonna send someone ter haul me load up the gangplank...I ain't got the muscle no more!"

"Yer never did 'ave any muscle as far as I remember, Sid Crewe, but as much as I'd like ter 'elp an old friend, Sid, yer surely must be aware of the seafaring rules!"

Sid hunched his puny shoulders with a vague look about him. "What yer bleedin' talkin' 'bout?"

"I ain't taking no petticoat onboard me ship, Crewe...It's the golden rule! They bring nought but bad luck!"

"Don't be so bleedin' superstitious, yer sounds more like some old biddy than a heroic skipper, besides, she's in a crate!"

"Don't fancy being strung up on the gallows fer murder an' all, Sid! She'll never survive the journey inside that wooden box!"

"Yer owes me, Felix Willow, yer said so yerself!" There was an uncomfortable silence, Felix had promised him a favour but he'd been stupid not to ask more details before agreeing and now he felt under pressure to comply. With his neck beginning to ache from continuously looking up at Felix, Sid suddenly had an idea that might just convince Felix Willow to have a change of heart.

"You 'ad the misfortune ov seeing that bleedin', Forbes lately, Felix?"

"Ah! don't mention that bleedin' sly cove, he's had me done up like a bleedin' kipper, more than once! It's a damned good job that I managed ter bribe me way out ov being arrested! Forbes is a rascal an' a smooth one at that...got his spies on every bleedin' corner an' in every tavern in the East End, waiting ter grass us 'ard working folk up! Thought it were bad enuff when bleedin' Edward Jackson, was top ov the pecking order, but I'll say this fer 'im, 'e was a liar an' a cheat, but 'e weren't no bleedin' sneaky snake, like bleedin' Buster Forbes!"

Sid took a deep puff on his clay pipe, inwardly pleased with Felix Willow's angry response to his inquiry.

"Anyway, Crewe, what's it ter you?"

"Let's just say that, you'll be right amused on yer return...can't spout no more, 'specially wiv yer being up there; like yer said, yer never know who's 'iding  in the shadows!"

Intrigued by what he was hearing, Felix reluctantly agreed in allowing the crate onto his ship, but clandestinely had no intention of it sailing across the Atlantic with him. As he warned Sid that he'd better not be tricking him, two of his shipmates were ordered to load the unusual cargo aboard The Golden Moon.

"God speed, Captain Willow!" bellowed Sid above the deafening clang of the anchor being raised, relieved that he'd finally got rid of the conspicuous crate before its contents began screaming for all to hear.

A quick and mocking salute was all Felix Willow could offer. He was late for his departure, the winds didn't appear in his favour and he already feared that the girl had jinxed his trip. He knew he'd be unable to relax until he'd got shot of her.

***********

Overcome with emotion after saying goodbye to Elizabeth, Peggy was left tearful and exhausted. She had failed in persuading her daughter not to leave England in such haste, with a graphic lecture of how different her life would be in India but, in the end, was forced to give in to Elizabeth Jackson's unbreakable strong will.

It had also been a gruelling day for Rayne; on any normal day, her signs of guilt would not have been overlooked by her empathetic grandmother. Tommy had still not shown up which was Rayne's main concern and with every scenario consuming her thoughts, she was of little comfort to Peggy in her hour of need. Peggy heeded to the only words of advice which Rayne had offered and retired early with a cup of hot milk laced with whiskey, to aid her sleep. Left alone with her fears, Rayne was becoming more convinced that, as usual, Tommy had acted foolishly and not followed her strict instructions to the latter. The painful knot in her stomach only seemed to tighten as she worried that Tommy had uncovered her lies. As the hands on the clock reached midnight, Rayne decided to call it a day and for the first time in her life, topped up her milk with whiskey and took to her bed.

************

The Salty Dog inn was about to close for the night and as Sid Crewe kept himself to himself, the adrenalin rushed through his veins, keeping all traits of tiredness at bay. Puffing hard on his clay pipe, he'd sipped his ale slowly throughout the evening, telling himself that he'd celebrate in true style once his mission was completed. He sniggered, remembering the bounty which would soon be his, not to mention how his scheme would affect Buster Forbes. He was the last to leave the alehouse and dawdled along the dockside, biding his time until the streets would be deserted. Pleased that The Golden Moon had set sail, he was already considering going underground for a long stretch, to avoid paying Felix Willow his due when he returned. The annoying squeak of his barrow echoed in the sleepy streets as he made his way towards Peggy's Grocery. Unable to wipe the smug grin from his face, he prayed that the, not so innocent, fiddle girl was now in dreamland as he pulled out the key from his pocket. As quiet as a mouse, he stood inside the shop, listening for sounds of movement or voices. The clock ticked noisily, disturbing his concentration. Lighting just one candle, Sid began loading the boxes of whiskey onto his cart and was soon left in a sweat. Pleased that the remainder of the boxes were much lighter, he hastily stripped the shop bare, causing his cart to become precariously overloaded. Not satisfied that he'd taken enough for one evening's work, Sid crept through to the parlour. Knowing that most of the older women hid their money in empty tins, jars or teapots, he set about opening every container he could find until, at last, he stumbled upon a far larger box of treasure than he could ever have anticipated. A biscuit tin with a handful of half-crowns and shillings, covering an envelope which was stuffed with a wad of crisp five-pound notes. Sid's mouth gaped open wide and his heart suddenly beat louder than the clock as he pondered over the endless possibilities that his discovery could offer him. He was a rich man. He could move out of the slum he called home, and live his days out like a true gent, he mused. He couldn't remember the last time he'd ever felt so euphoric and for a brief moment toyed with the idea of abandoning the loaded cart and just taking the money, but he was a greedy man by nature and already had more than enough folk in mind who would be interested in buying the merchandise. After stuffing his pockets full with the money, he snatched the butter dish from the table, hoping a rub of butter would put an end to his cart's squeaky wheels. Taking a hurried last look around the bare shop, Sid was about to blow out the candle when he was suddenly alerted to the sound of voices. Convinced they were coming from upstairs, his spontaneous reaction was to use the flame of the candle to set fire to the pile of paper bags on the shop's counter and create a decoy while he made a quick getaway. Not quite out of Whitechapel Street, Sid glanced back over his shoulder where he viewed the bright orange flames from the burning inferno. Feeling the strain from every muscle in his puny body as he pushed the heavy costermonger's cart, a brilliant idea suddenly flitted through Sid Crewe's devious mind.

"Folk don't call me *the scavenger* fer nought," he declared to himself, triumphantly, as he took a deep breath in the hope of gaining some physical strength. Infused with determination and with his head down, Sid hurried to his lodging room in Gunthorpe Street; a damp and dilapidated terrace, where at least eight overburdened families were packed in like rats and seemed to breed like them too. The walls were constantly damp and dripping with black mould and the overpowering aroma of decay never faded, seeming to adhere to every nook and cranny of the building. Sid's minute living area was, in fact, only a third of one divided room, but since he lived alone it was spacious in comparison to his fellow lodger's accommodation and thankfully it was on the ground floor.

After securing his hoard, Sid opened a bottle of the fine whiskey, gulping it back thirstily before concealing it in the oversized pocket of his jacket and stepping back out onto the street, making his way towards Commercial Street and Forbes Entertainment Hall. 'This is gonna be a bleedin' night yer won't ferget in an 'urry, Buster *'big shot'* Forbes!' he muttered as he lit his pipe. 'I'll teach yer a bleedin' lesson an' knock yer off yer high 'orse.'

# CHAPTER TWENTY-TWO

*The Golden Moon* dropped anchor at Woolwich docks, a port now closed for commercial use and taken over by the military. Beneath the obscure veil of darkness, Felix Willow was confident that he could quickly drop off his unwanted load and sail away without being spotted. The distant sound of high spirited, drunken sailors, however, stirred up twinges of guilt, giving Felix second thoughts about abandoning the young and vulnerable lass upon the quayside. Having already lost too much time, he felt it would be as much of an ill omen to leave Edward Jackson's daughter in the hands of the untrustworthy naval cadets as it would be to have her on board, so he instructed his two junior shipmates to make haste and deliver the unwanted cargo to the first house they arrived at. The crate was gently hoisted down the port side as the young lads scurried down the knotted rope, nervously fearing the presence of any guard who might be lurking in the darkness. They kept silent and trod cautiously, while Felix Willow kept vigil on deck. Sid Crewe's incompetent accomplice had kept the chloroform soaked rag tied tightly around Tilly's mouth, and she remained dangerously out cold. Arriving in a dimly lit, narrow, cobbled street where a row of tiny cottages was situated, the young lads quietly agreed that it appeared to be a safe area and following Captain's orders, abandoned the crate and made a dash back to the awaiting ship.

*************

As the striking of the clock tower echoed throughout Whitechapel, three o'clock seemed the perfect time for Sid to put his next devious plan into action. The drunkards and harlots had vanished for another day and it felt as though the entire world was in a state of deep slumber during the short interval before the costermongers would once again begin another working day. To Sid's astonishment, the double doors to the music hall were still unlocked; he wondered if perhaps Tommy was still at work, he'd not seen him earlier, he pondered. He furtively pushed one of the doors open, just enough to squeeze his puny body in through the narrow gap. He stood motionless, holding his breath and squinting his watchful eyes. There was only silence. Deciding to take a quick tour of the building he entered the admissions kiosk and pocketed the bunch of keys, the evening's takings were still in the drawer which convinced Sid that Tommy must still be on the premises; maybe he'd fallen asleep somewhere, he considered. He filled his pockets with the tempting, loose change before continuing. The large hall was stuffy and the pungent combination of lingering smoke, body odour, cheap perfume and vomit persuaded Sid to move on quickly. He couldn't understand how anyone could gain pleasure from an evening spent in such an atmosphere, being entertained by a gang of out of tune amateurs. He continued his tour, room by room, but there wasn't a soul anywhere to be found. Downstairs, the dressing rooms were empty and as he reached the very depths of the building he entered the fiddle girl's dressing room, sniggering to himself as he viewed its filth and mess. 'If only folk knew the truth about the angelic, sweet little fiddle girl!' he muttered under his breath. His eyes caught sight of the overfull waste paper bin; the perfect place to start a fire he decided as he quickly struck a match. It took little time before the metal bin was ablaze, he kicked it over and threw the hanging clothes onto its flames before smashing the paraffin lamp alongside it. A small explosion immediately illuminated the dressing room, with the ball of fire causing Sid to leap back up the stairs, two at a time. Out of breath, he casually closed the music hall doors behind him and marched along the empty street, proud of his evening's achievements.

\*\*\*\*\*\*\*\*\*\*\*\*

Woken by his reoccurring nightmare, Cecil Berry had been gazing up at the night sky from his bedroom window, desperately hoping to see his mother's face amongst the magical stars, when the two men, carrying a huge crate, suddenly caught his eye. With his face now squashed up against the windowpane, he was quite sure that the crate had been left outside of his front door, even though the jutting stone, window ledge obscured his vision. Anxious to investigate further, he pondered whether on not he should go and wake his pa or his granny, knowing they'd likely be cross with him. But his excitement and curiosity far exceeded his fear of being scolded. Cecil sat quietly for a while, staring at his pa, who was breathing heavily in a deep sleep on the opposite side of their room. Tiptoeing from his bed, he knelt down, positioning his face close to his pa's face.

"*Pa!*" He said, in a loud whisper. "Pa! Are you awake?"

Ralph Berry opened one eye, "Of course I'm not awake, lad, it's the middle of the night. Go back to your bed an' let your pa sleep!"

"*Pa!* I saw two men and they left a massive crate outside our front door...I'm *really, really* sure they did!"

"Hmmm, you've been dreaming son!" groaned Ralph, pulling the blanket over his head.

"Can I go and tell Granny then? Would that be alright, Pa...*please!*"

Ralph sat up, feeling his heart contract as his son's similarities to his beloved Elsie, seemed to jump out at him. At only six years old, Cecil was growing more like his mother with every passing year; identical almond-shaped, green eyes, as dark as the forest and his thick, lower lip with its slight pout, exactly as Elsie's had been. As he stared hard at his motherless son, he could hear Elsie's softly spoken voice cajoling him not to ignore their son. In their seven years of marriage, he'd never once heard Elsie raise her voice, she was the gentlest of women, almost angelic in her conduct.

"Pa! I saw two men and they left a present for us! I was looking for Ma's face in the stars and wishing for her! Maybe..."

"Ah, lad, such wishes don't come true, your beautiful ma is up in Heaven now...you might catch a glimpse of her loveliness in amongst the night stars, but that's as far as it goes son; you'll only upset yourself by wishing for more. Now come along, I can see that if I want another wink of sleep tonight, I'm gonna have to go and take a look outside...reckon you were just dreaming, Cecil! Folk around here aren't in the habit of dropping off gifts!"

*"I wasn't dreaming Pa!"* protested Cecil, as he searched under his pa's bed for his slippers.

"Well, you stay here, son, I don't want Granny woken up at this hour!"

It came as a huge shock to discover that Cecil hadn't merely dreamt about the wooden crate. Ralph viewed it cautiously before making a hasty decision to drag it into the cramped hallway; if there was something worth keeping, he didn't want to risk any of his neighbours being in on it. He predicted that it was likely to be a smugglers hoard, abandoned in their hurried escape. Finding it too heavy and bulky for him to lift, Ralph eased the crate over the stone step and pushed it far enough to enable him to close the front door again. The odour of chloroform was immediately apparent, alarming Ralph that this was not a crate of contraband, before him. Hearing his pa struggling, Cecil couldn't stop himself from disobeying him and was soon sat halfway down the stairs watching with intrigue as his pa quickly prised out the nails and lifted the lid.

"What's inside Pa? It smells funny...can I come down?"

Ralph didn't answer but hastily pulled at the stained blanket, already knowing that inside was a body. He turned the crate onto its side, enabling him to drag out the bundle. The sudden fear that he was about to unveil a corpse caused him to yell at Cecil.

*"Get to your bedroom, lad! Don't disobey your father!"*

Feeling his eyes burning, Cecil blinked away his tears as he scurried up the stairs straight into the arms of his granny who'd been woken from all the disturbance.

"What on earth is going on, for heaven's sake?" she exclaimed.

"It's a box of treasure, granny! I saw the two

men who left it outside for us!"

"Take him to his bed, Mother!" cried Ralph.

"This is *no* treasure I assure you! For the love of God, shield his young eyes and mind!"

Ruth Berry immediately sensed what the crate contained and did as her son requested, much to Cecil's annoyance.

As the pungent odour of chloroform became more intense, Tilly's pretty face was soon visible. Wasting no time, Ralph cut the soaked gag and unravelled the blanket, quickly discarding them to the backyard. He proceeded to liberally rinse her face and neck with cool water, wanting to wash away all traces of the lethal chemical. Within minutes, Tilly opened her eyes and gasped for pure air. With a sigh of relief, Ralph called out to his mother to bring him a blanket.

"Where am I?" were Tilly's first words.

"You're safe... and no harm will come to you under my roof!"

With every bone in her weakened body aching and her head pounding, Tilly had an innate feeling that the man before her spoke words of truth. After drifting in and out of consciousness, fearing that she was to be thrown into the sea or even buried alive, Tilly's overwhelming sense of relief moved her to tears. She had suffered more than most young women throughout her twenty-one years, but during the last few weeks, she felt as though she'd been to hell, never to return.

With all efforts proving unsuccessful in saving Peggy's Grocery from total destruction, Rayne sat on the pavement of Whitechapel Street with her head buried in her hands, sobbing her heart and soul out and wishing she'd been taken from the world, just as her dear grandmamma had been. Deep down she knew that it was entirely her fault that such a devastating disaster had taken place. How could she ever forgive herself? How could she ever taste a day of happiness again after this, were the statements dominating her thoughts? The smouldering ruin behind her would be sure to reappear in her dreams every night and as neighbours insisted that she should accept their offers of hospitality and vacate the pavement, Rayne felt the need to punish herself more by remaining next to the grim scene of torment. Completely oblivious to the fact that a couple of streets away, Forbes music hall had also been reduced to a pile of ashes along with two neighbouring warehouses, Rayne wondered if the word on the street had yet reached Buster Forbes and Tommy, she prayed that they might soon show up and ease her sorrows with their sympathy and compassion.

# CHAPTER TWENTY-THREE

Torn between accompanying Tommy to London or staying by Eleanor's side, August was unsure as to whether he could trust Tommy with such a delicate mission. He knew how manipulative Rayne could be, especially when it concerned Tommy Kettle, but at the same time, he also knew that he had to simply trust that, Tommy had learnt his lesson and wouldn't allow Rayne to sweet talk him anymore. He had been infuriated when discovering the copious lies she'd spun. Tommy now knew for certain that Rayne didn't have any feelings for him and certainly didn't have any intentions of becoming his wife. Eleanor had developed a high temperature during the night, and with the local doctor still nowhere in sight, no matter how much Eleanor pleaded with August to rescue Tilly, his inner senses were screaming at him to ignore her pleas and remain close by her side. How could he possibly walk away from his beloved Eleanor while she was so weak and in such a delicate condition, he mused, knowing how he'd never forgive himself should her situation deteriorate in his absence. The entire household plus Peggy and Winifred were all in agreement that he should put his trust in Tommy to bring Tilly home safely; when all was said and done, they had stressed,  Whitechapel

was Tommy's home ground and if there proved
to be a tricky situation, August's unfamiliar face
might hinder any rescue attempt not to mention
affect Rayne's behaviour.

With an ear full of instructions and a pocket full
of money to cover his costs, Tommy headed off
in the direction of Oxford's railway station
whilst August prayed that he was doing the
right thing.

Fuelled by anger and deep in thought, Tommy
took long strides as he repeatedly rehearsed
what he would do and say after he'd freed poor
Tilly and stood before Rayne announcing that
her real half-sister was in Oxford, married to
August Miller and expecting his child. His mind
was so preoccupied that his return journey home
passed by quickly. A rush of adrenalin pumping
through his veins infused him with a surge of
uncharacteristic confidence, he felt courageous
and ready to tackle the devious mind of Rayne
Jackson.

The unusual crowd in Commercial Street at such
an early hour immediately told him that all was
not well; there was an overpowering stench in
the air that outweighed the pungent summer
aroma of the Thames. He increased his pace and
as he suddenly caught sight of Buster Forbes,
heading towards him, the alarming sight of the
gaping section where, only yesterday, the music
hall had stood, stole away his confidence in the
splitting of a second.

Tommy had never in his entire life witnessed such a steely look of exasperation upon Buster Forbes' face, he felt his bowels contract and wanted to turn around and run, but Forbes was making a determined beeline straight towards him.

*"Where the Hell 'ave you been, Kettle?* What's been going on for Gawd's sake! The entire building 'as been burnt ter the ground!" Forbes had hold of Tommy's arm as he screamed in his face, a purple vein bulging across his forehead.

"I dunno Gov! 'onest, I just got back from Oxf'rd!"

"I don't bleedin' well pay yer wages and kit yer out in them fancy togs so as yer can go swannin' off ter bleedin' Oxf'rd at the drop of a hat! *Where's Rayne?"*

"I dunno, Gov!" said Tommy, his small voice quivering. "I guess she went 'ome afore the fire started...*Oh no!* There's a young woman in there, Mister Forbes! She were tied up so there weren't no way she could 'ave escaped...oh bleedin 'ell, this is terrible...'ow am I gonna tell August an' is Misses?"

"Shut yer bleedin' pie 'ole, Tommy! I don't know what yer blabbing on about, but there was definitely nobody inside the building! Now let's go see what Rayne *bleedin'* Jackson 'as ter say fer 'erself!"

"She made me go ter Oxf'rd, gov...wanted me ter deliver a letter by 'and! She ain't ter be trusted, Gov! She's even 'ad 'er half-sister tied up down in 'er dressing room fer weeks on end, but turns out she was the wrong girl!"

"Yer bin drinking, Kettle? Cos you're certainly ranting like a bleedin 'drunk an' yer ain't makin' no sense at all!"

"But it's true, Gov, I swear on me ma's life...Rayne got Sid Crewe ter kidnap 'er half-sister from Oxf'rd, but the idiot took the maid instead. All cos she's in love with her half-sister's 'usband, *August Miller!*"

Buster suddenly came to an abrupt halt; the devastating sight of where Peggy's Grocery had stood was now in sight; he couldn't believe his eyes.

"***Bleedin' 'eck!***" cried Tommy. "Not a novver bleedin' fire!"

Buster increased his pace, as he spotted Rayne, who was still sat on the pavement, red-eyed and weeping into her palms.

"Oh, Mr Forbes!" she cried in despair. "My Grandmamma couldn't get out in time! She's dead, Mr Forbes and I'm left all alone in the world!"

They were the declarations of a selfish coward, considered Buster as he looked down on the spoilt 'fiddle girl' with contempt. He doubted she'd even tried to save the poor old woman and if what Tommy had said proved true, she had a lot to answer for. He had lost far too much in the space of one evening, and an innocent old woman had died, many more folk would now be out of a job and then there was the kidnapped maid. Buster had a gnawing feeling that Rayne Jackson was behind every disaster, and she dared to have the audacity to sit in the gutter feeling sorry for herself.

"My music hall is also smouldering away, *Rayne*...did you know that?"

Rayne took in a sharp breath, clearly shocked by the news. "*Oh no! That's dreadful!*"

"*Your half-sister was inside, Rayne!*" roared Tommy, urgently.

Letting her guard down, Rayne appeared smug, "Oh don't worry about *her*, dearest Tommy! She's probably halfway across the Atlantic by now! Did you deliver my letter, Tommy?"

"Yeah, and I spoke ter, August Miller, *an'* ter 'is new wife!"

"Don't be foolish, Tommy, August didn't really marry another...I was merely pulling your leg...you must have been mistaken! You probably saw a maid and as they say, *put two and two together!*"

"What d'yer mean, that she's 'alfway 'cross the Atlantic by now, Rayne! What 'ave yer gone an' done!"

"Please don't fret over that gold-digging, illegitimate guttersnipe! She isn't worth the rags which clothe her! Now, Tommy, be a sweetheart and find me somewhere to stay while I get over the tragic loss of poor Grandmamma!"

*"Rayne Jackson!* find yer own bleedin' bed ter kip in, cos I'm going ter search fer that poor lass! Yer nought but a heartless bitch, Rayne! Does that bleedin' scavenger 'ave anyfing ter do wiv yer nasty 'andy work?"

*"Get lost, Tommy!* You're a bigger fool than you look if you thought, for one minute, that there was ever the slightest chance that you had a future with me! I'm sure Mr Forbes will take good care of me until I sort myself out and bury poor Grandmamma! He's a *proper* gentleman!"

Buster Forbes, who had listened on in silence was utterly sickened by Rayne's callous behaviour, and as fragile and innocent as she might appear, he now considered her to be a slippery, heartless snake, not to be trusted.

"Well, that's where yer mistaken, Miss Jackson! It is blatantly clear ter me that you've inherited yer father's heart of stone and in my opinion, you have reaped the ugly harvest from your own devious sowing and I want nothing more ter do with you, and furthermore, if anything has 'appened ter that poor lass who yer kept prisoner, then you'll soon be feelin' the hangman's noose, squeezing the life out ov yer!"

Finally deciding to stand up to face Buster and Tommy, Rayne already had a plan and felt she had nothing to lose in her conduct towards the two barking hounds. "Don't think I can't survive without your help...you're both equally revolting. You deserve everything you got,

*Buster Forbes,* and I'm only sorry that my darling Pappa didn't slaughter you when he ruled the streets of Whitechapel...according to my grandma's accounts, you were simply his obedient lapdog, just as Tommy has been my, eager to please, puppy since I arrived in this awful place! There is a most congenial man, worth ten of you two, in Oxford and I know he will be absolutely delighted when I waltz into his lonely life!"

*"No!"* exclaimed Tommy, as he tried to control his anger. "August Miller despises you more than we do! And he and Eleanor are awaiting the arrival of their first child ...you would not be welcome there, in fact, if you go anywhere near Oxford you will be arrested on charges of abduction! They know everything about your evil plans, Rayne and I read every one of your pathetic love letters. You are nothing but an enemy to them!"

In a state of confusion, Rayne was left speechless as she mused over Tommy's words.

"You had the wrong lass in your dressing room, Rayne!" added Buster. "It would seem that yer ain't quite as clever as yer pa was!"

*"You're lying!"* she screamed, hysterically. "That's impossible, she would have said if she wasn't Eleanor!"

"Some folks 'ave beating hearts in their chests, Rayne, hearts which have genuine unconditional love infused within them, and Tilly kept silent about her true identity because of her true sisterly love for your real, half-sister and that's why I'm not gonna rest 'til I've found 'er and taken 'er back ter Oxf'rd, where she belongs an' where she is adored." Tommy puffed out his chest, feeling proud of his declaration.

"I'll 'elp yer, Tommy lad, it's the least I can do, an' then maybe I might just find another job for yer! We'll begin with that good fer nothing, Sid Crewe: I've got a sneaky feeling that he's at the bottom of all this and probably took his orders from *her!*"

"What about me! You can't simply abandon me here! What would my Grandmamma have said, Mr Forbes, she trusted you to look out for me! Think of that!"

Buster Forbes laughed out loud. "Try playing a tune on yer fiddle! Come along now Tommy, we've got some serious  detective work waiting ter be solved!"

As Buster and Tommy turned their backs on her, Rayne was left screaming at the top of her voice, like a lunatic. "But I don't even have a violin anymore! What will become of me! I will be ruined! Everyone has abandoned me! It's not fair! You can't just walk away from me! Tommy, come back, I promise to never lie to you again! Please, Tommy! *Please!*"

# CHAPTER TWENTY-FOUR

The tiny backyard of number three, Antelope Street was a sun trap drenched with the sweet fragrance of pink and white climbing roses which stretched their thorny branches almost to the peak of the towering, whitewashed walls. Now one of Tilly's favourite places in her temporary home, she soaked up the warmth of the continuous July sunshine as she eagerly waited for her day to quickly pass and for the return of Ralph Berry. Following the day when he had so tenderly bathed her face and whispered his kind assuring words in her ears, she knew that she had fallen in love with him. Never before had such intense feelings seized her heart in such a peculiar way; it wasn't at all like the days when she lived in the workhouse and had reminisced over the lad who attended church most Sundays. She now knew what true love felt like; it was a potent force, mightier than anything she'd ever been acquainted with throughout her entire life. When she was in Ralph's company, it felt as though time had been sped up; her heartbeat became suddenly wild and rowdy within her chest and she so desperately yearned for the minutes to last forever, but when he was away at work, time came to an agonising halt, leaving her with such a longing that she felt almost crippled by its pain. She would look deep into his eyes during every conversation in the hope of gaining some kind of response from him, always mulling over in her thoughts whether he'd been so deeply in love with his late wife that, even after five years of her departing the world, he was still unable to love another woman. She had also grown fond of young Cecil, who she sensed was delighted in having a young and more motherly figure in his life. Both Ruth and Ralph had mentioned how his nightmares had ceased since her arrival. Even when Tilly felt recovered enough to travel back to Oxford, she furtively made out that she continued to suffer from bouts of fatigue and muscle pain in her legs, unable to face saying goodbye to Ralph. The mere thought of it never failed to make her eyes well up and she knew that her heart would shatter into pieces if a romance failed to ignite between them. Everything about Ralph was tender and kind, he wasn't like so many boisterous and loud-mouthed men she'd observed throughout her life, a tailor by profession, he would often bring some work home to complete, reminding her of Austin Hyde, another true and trustworthy gentleman. Tilly had told Ruth and Ralph everything about her life, and about the people with who she shared it with, in Paradise Street. They had listened intently during the evenings and she now worried that perhaps she'd spoken so passionately about her life in Oxford that it may have prevented Ralph from opening up about any feelings he might harbour for her, sensing how she wished to recuperate from her ordeal and return to Oxford as soon as possible. Did he feel the same odd sensation as she did, when their hands accidentally brushed together, she mused? Did he yearn to hold her in his embrace as she longed to feel his arms wrap around her and his body close to hers? These were the thoughts that kept her awake until the early hours of the morning and caused a painful knot to cramp her stomach by day. Tilly now knew the meaning of the word love-sick, an ailment which she'd always been adamant didn't exist.

Knowing that she couldn't drag out her stay for much longer and with Eleanor's confinement rapidly approaching, Tilly was in a quandary as to how she should handle the delicate situation. She had written to Eleanor in the first instant after being rescued, assuring her that she was in the best of hands and how the kind Mr Berry would escort her home when she was well enough. Now, four weeks and ten letters later, she had confided in Ellie about her true feelings for the widower, apologising for not being by Ellie's side during her needful time. Ellie had been quick in reassuring Tilly that she had more than enough people fussing over her, jokingly writing how she felt tempted to join her dear sister in Woolwich for some peace and quiet.

Ellie prayed that Tilly would not return to Oxford with a broken heart, she deserved the love and devotion of a good man and a taste of the joy which had filled her own life since she'd been reunited with August.

"Can you live with us forever?" asked Cecil, one Sunday afternoon, as they all relaxed over a pot of tea and a slice of one of Tilly's sponge cakes.
"Cecil!" admonished Ruth and Ralph in unison. Ralph and Tilly's eyes met, and as usual, she felt her heart skip a beat. She was sure he had feelings for her too, but was somehow afraid to voice them. Was it because of Cecil she wondered, did he presume that she would want nothing to do with a man who already had a son?
"Cecil, you are one of the sweetest boys I've ever met, and I'm going to be truly heartbroken to leave your lovely home and your kind pa and grandma, but I'm sure we can still meet from time to time; Oxford isn't too far away, you know."
"But it won't be the same, Tilly...will it?"
"That's enough now, young man!" ordered Ruth, issuing Cecil with a stern, warning glare. As Cecil buried his face in a cushion, everyone knew that he was hiding his tears.
"There's no hurry Tilly," assured Ralph, "as I've stressed many a time, you are welcome to stay for as long as you wish and until you feel fully

recovered, and regained your strength."

"Did you ever hear what became of that awful Rayne girl?" asked Ruth, purposely changing the subject.

"I did, as a matter of fact. In her most recent letter, Ellie wrote of how the police had failed to find that vile man who'd kidnapped me and tried to send me to the other side of the world, but that Rayne had spun a tale as to how he'd forced her at knifepoint to assist him! She seemed to have got off completely free of any blame, and has since embarked on a voyage to India to join her mother, where, I pray she will remain for the rest of her life! I hope I never have to set eyes on her again and I know Ellie feels the same, regardless of her being her half-sister!"

"She certainly sounds like a rotten apple to me," agreed, Ruth. "Maybe her mother will be able to teach her a thing or two!"

"Apparently, Tommy Kettle, who now corresponds with August Miller, told him that Rayne's mother had given her grandmother a large sum of money before she set sail; it was for their shipping costs should they ever decide to join her in India, but it was obviously destroyed in the fire and Rayne's mother refused to reimburse her, so Rayne had to borrow a violin and practically fiddle non-stop until she'd earned enough to pay for her passage!"

"A small punishment for the amount of

suffering she's caused!" expressed Ruth, shaking her head in disbelief.

"Pa, can we play catch in the backyard?"

"Ooh, look at the time!" declared Ruth. "I promised I'd take afternoon tea with Mr Page!"

"You already had afternoon tea, Granny!" voiced Cecil.

"Another one won't hurt me, sweetheart; now run along and find your ball and let poor Tilly enjoy a peaceful Sunday afternoon!"

As Ralph tossed and caught the ball with his son, his mind was heavily preoccupied; how would he cope after Tilly had returned to Oxford? She had been like a glowing beacon in his dull life over the past few weeks. He never, in a thousand years, ever thought he could love again after Elsie, but it was as though Tilly had been left outside of his home by the angels, a gift to treasure, a new beginning, and he was unable to untangle his tongue and speak the words which were bursting out from his heart. Why would a pretty young woman wish to marry a man ten years older and with a family already, he mused.

"*Butterfingers!*" yelled Cecil, bringing him out of his reverie.

"You're catching more balls than me son, good job it's not a cricket match!"

"You've dropped it eight times now, Pa! I've been counting! And I only dropped it two times!"

"You mean twice, Cecil! Well, maybe we should ask Tilly if she'd like to be on my side since I'm such a butterfingers today!"

"But granny said..."

"Just go and ask her, Cecil, tell her your pa needs some support!"

Delighted to be asked to join in the fun, fond memories of Charlie sprung to her mind; she did miss him and young Felicity so much and hoped that in her absence they'd not forgotten her.

"I can tell you've played this game before!" joked Ralph as he continued to purposely drop the ball, thrilled by the proud look upon Cecil's face as he caught nearly every ball thrown at him.

"I have indeed, Mr Berry, but it would seem that you require a lot of practice!"

"My pa, has got butterfingers today!" giggled Cecil.

"He needs lots of help!" laughed Tilly, her cheeks rosy from the heat, "I suggest he should be on my side and whoever drops the ball more than five times is out of the competition!"

"I'm going to win!" cried Cecil, joyfully.

During the next fifteen minutes, the game continued with Tilly and Ralph clandestinely determined to let Cecil be victorious as they both purposely continued to drop the ball. Their hands fleetingly brushed together as they both attempted to pick up the ball at the same time.

The brief encounter caused their smiling faces to be replaced by a deep and serious gaze. Overwhelmed by an instant shyness, Tilly swiftly diverted her glance. The unique moment seemed to have briefly brought time to a standstill and as much as Ralph wanted to declare his feelings for Tilly, his tongue became momentarily paralysed. When it came to affairs of the heart, he was no longer the confident man of years ago. He was out of practice and convinced that he would only be met by words of rejection, leaving him to feel humiliated.

"That's it, son!" announced Ralph, "you've definitely triumphed in this game! *Well done!*"

"Yes, well done, Cecil!" Tilly repeated, sensing that Ralph had cut short the game.

Claiming a headache, for the remainder of the afternoon, Tilly shut herself away in Ruth Berry's bedroom where her palliasse occupied the corner of the tiny room. Her mind was in a quandary; she was in love with Ralph Berry and although she sometimes sensed that he harboured similar feelings towards her, she was growing more convinced that he must have promised himself never to love another after his wife's death and she felt it would be the kindest favour for her to bring forward her return date to Oxford and put the inhabitants of Antelope Street out of her heart and mind. While she remained under their roof, she considered, she was only inflicting torture on herself and possibly Ralph too. Besides, she consoled herself, Eleanor would soon become a mother and require her sisterly support; there would be plenty to do in Paradise Street to keep her mind occupied; she missed everyone so much too, the mere thought of her extended family brought on a sudden rush of homesickness. It was decided, she asserted; she would inform the Berry family of her wish to return to Oxford over supper that very evening.

# CHAPTER TWENTY-FIVE

The tranquil atmosphere around the dining table fell into a sudden decline, the moment Tilly announced her intentions to return to Oxford. Admonished by his father for bursting into tears and causing Tilly to feel guilty for wanting to leave, Cecil's miserable face only added to the gloom.

 "Tilly has her own family and a life in Oxford to return to, Cecil!" declared Ralph in an aloof tone before stating how he had to check on something in the tailor's shop, where he was employed. Cecil begged to accompany him, hoping that he could persuade his pa into convincing Tilly to stay a little longer, but in his concealed annoyance and with his heart aching in a way which it hadn't felt since he was in mourning for Elsie, five years ago, Ralph ordered his son to go to bed.

Fully aware that her son was nursing an aching heart, Ruth wondered if perhaps he'd received a rejection from Tilly earlier that day. Since the first week of Tilly's arrival, she had harboured a strong motherly sense that Ralph was falling in love with the delightfully, sweet lass. Who couldn't adore such a kind-hearted and loving young woman, she mused, she would make the perfect wife for Ralph, and she had a wonderful way with Cecil, who clearly adored her too.

"Do I *have* to go to bed now, Granny! I'm not
even tired and there's no sign of the moon or the
stars!" begged Cecil, after hearing the front door
slam.

Ruth smiled lovingly at her grandson, as she
cupped his dimpled chin in her hand, "Go and
play out the back for half an hour, my darling,
but don't expect to stay up until the moon
appears because that would be far too late!"
Spontaneously kissing his granny's cheek, Cecil
skipped happily out of the room before she
changed her mind.

"Did something happen while I was taking
afternoon tea with Mr Page?" asked Ruth, in a
casual manner.

Feeling her cheeks warm up, Tilly was shocked
by Mrs Berry's direct question.

"I'm not quite sure what you mean, Mrs Berry!"
Ruth brushed some imaginary crumbs from off
the pristine, white table cloth, as she chose her
words carefully. Had she read the signs
wrongly, she wondered? She prided herself in
being able to detect love when it was
blossoming, but perhaps this was a situation too
close to home and young Tilly had arrived in
such a weak and vulnerable state, maybe she
was reading something far too ambiguous into
the situation.

"I'll come straight to the point, Tilly, because I
believe you are a young woman not unlike
myself and prefer to hear things direct and as

they stand! Are you in love with my son?"
Her frankness threw Tilly; she felt a giddy
sensation as she sat staring in disbelief with her
mind oddly drifting from the topic. She found
herself thinking how youthful Ruth Berry
appeared; far too young-looking to be called
*Granny*, she pondered, concluding that she must
have been a young bride and had born Ralph
nine months later. Sensing that Ruth was
becoming impatient waiting for an answer, Tilly
fidgeted in the chair, before making eye contact
and confidently launching into her
proclamation, "*Yes*, Mrs Berry, I *do* love Ralph; in
truth, I love him very deeply as I have never
loved before; he fills my entire heart! But, sadly,
I doubt he harbours the same feelings towards
me!"
Tilly's declaration was music to Ruth's ears, and
knowing that the seeds of love had already been
sown, she knew it would now be up to her to
nurture them into full bloom.
 "Does Ralph have any inkling of your feelings,
Tilly?"
 "I thought, perhaps, he did, but now I'm not so
sure...I get a distinct feeling that he's holding
back, but then I'm no expert in such matters and
admit that this is my first real experience of
loving a man and wishing so desperately for my
emotions to be recognised!"
 "Nothing would please me more than to have
you as my daughter in law, Tilly! I believe you

would be the perfect match for my Ralph and you have a beautiful way with young Cecil, who undoubtedly adores you!"

A feeling of optimism swelled Tilly's heart, but she knew that no matter what Ruth Berry said, when all was said and done, it was up to Ralph to take the lead and in her opinion, for some unknown reason, he was reluctant. Maybe he didn't hold a torch for her, she pondered, maybe she'd simply imagined it and, as she'd just admitted to Mrs Berry, her knowledge and experience of affairs of the heart were very limited.

"Has he not given you any signs, Tilly? Has he not even attempted to admit to his feelings? I know he tends to be a bit coy sometimes. Have you mentioned anything of how you feel to him?"

"*Certainly not, Mrs Berry!* I have always held the strongest belief that it should be the man who is first to voice his declaration of love! That being, of course, that he actually has any! Ralph is a good ten years older than me, and he has been married before! He's not a young, bashful beau! No, Mrs Berry, I will return to Oxford in two days and with the help of my family, hopefully, get over my first experience of a broken heart. I will miss you, Mrs Berry, and young Cecil. I truly hope we can correspond with each other. I will never be able to thank you enough for all that you've done for me!"

"Oh Tilly, won't you stay for just another few weeks...just to see how things progress?"

"As much as I'd love to, Mrs Berry, it would be too painful and besides, Eleanor will be having her baby soon and I must be at her side, she has experienced such a distressful confinement because of all the trauma my abduction has caused... and I do miss her so much, Mrs Berry!"

"I can understand that, my dear, but I'm sure she'd be the first one to encourage you to stay a little longer; just enough for me to point out to my son how I detect there is love in the air and that he'd be a fool to let you slip out of his life!"

"I believe I have told you the story of how August spent two years searching for Ellie, Mrs Berry. Well, that is my vision of love too...I want Ralph to come to me..to woo me regardless of whether he believes I love him and until he acts accordingly, I can only presume that his heart does not welcome me into it...I hope you can comprehend my feelings, Mrs Berry!"

Ruth nodded silently, she knew exactly what Tllly meant and couldn't blame her at all.

"You must do what you see fit, Tilly, my dear, but remember this, you will always be welcomed with open arms in our home! We are all going to miss you so much, Tilly!"

With a painful lump in her throat, Tilly suddenly realised how Ruth Berry had become like a mother to her over the weeks, she had helped nurture her back to health, showing her such devotion and compassion which only a mother would display. She had never once enquired as to how long it would be until Tilly returned to Oxford, and had allowed Tilly to share her bedroom with her. Ruth clandestinely wiped away a stray tear before collecting the dishes from the table.

"*Let me do that!*" insisted Tilly, taking the dishes from Ruth's hands.

"God bless you, Tilly! I'll go and prise Cecil out of the yard and get him to bed before his pa comes home...I'm going to pray extra hard tonight that Ralph sees sense and doesn't let you slip out of our lives! I have the strongest of notions that you two were destined to become man and wife...and I'm not usually mistaken!"

Although they all tried to behave as though nothing had happened, during the following two days, there was an uncomfortable and strained atmosphere under the Berry's roof. Cecil had been warned, by his granny, not to continuously nag Tilly to stay, but he had stealthily whispered his desires in her ear when he thought the coast was clear. Tilly had assured him how she would write to him and had also said that if she was ever in London again, she would call in on Antelope Street, even though London had only filled her with a mixture of unpleasant memories and a broken heart.

Both Ruth and Tilly were unable to stem their flow of tears as they hugged each other goodbye in the tiny hallway.

"Take care of yourself, young Tilly, I wish things could have turned out different! I'm going to miss you so much!"

"Thank you for everything, Mrs Berry!" expressed Tilly, tearfully as she hurried into the waiting Hanson cab with Ralph.

Ruth silently prayed that during the short journey to Euston railway station, Ralph would muster up the courage and allow his heart to speak out.

They spoke of the clement July weather, of how Cecil now practised his ball-catching every day, joking that he might one day play cricket at the Oval ground. Tilly spoke of her excitement in being reunited with her many friends in Paradise Street, especially Ellie and the children and Ralph declared how he hoped one day to be in a similar position as Mr and Mrs Hyde and own his own tailor's shop.

As Euston railway station's distinctive, Bramley Fall, stone columns came into view, Tilly knew that Ralph had no intention of trying to persuade her to stay. She now knew that she'd been sadly mistaken, and any feelings of love on his side had merely been imagined. Ralph Berry didn't love her and she warned herself to be strong and not to shed a single tear during their parting words.

"Are you certain I cant accompany you on the journey to Oxford, Tilly?" bellowed Ralph above the deafening hullabaloo from the arriving and departing locomotives. "It seems rather ungentlemanly, in my opinion!"

"I'll be perfectly fine, Ralph, you have done more than enough for me already and remember, I've lived in the workhouse, been homeless and forced to sleep on the banks of the river, and been kidnapped and held prisoner! Not to mention being drugged and shoved into a wooden crate! A scenic train journey will be pleasant, to say the least!"

Ralph stared hard at the brave and beautiful young lass who had succeeded in doing what he deemed to be impossible for the rest of his life. Was he actually going to simply wave her off and let her disappear from his life? Why couldn't he say what his heart was screaming out to him? What was wrong with him? He questioned, as he felt a gloomy shadow slowly flutter down upon him and darken his vision.

"Goodbye, Tilly!"

"Goodbye, Ralph, and thank you!"

Left standing in a thick plume of smoke, Ralph stood motionless as the colossal locomotive chugged its way vociferously along the tracks and disappeared from his sight. Oblivious to the crowds on the platform, he released a guttural cry of despair as the taste of his salty tears wetted his lips.

# CHAPTER TWENTY-SIX

"I've got an overpowering feeling that today is going to be a wonderful day, my darling!" Eleanor had woken up in the most euphoric of moods and was buzzing with energy. There was a long list of jobs that she wanted to attend to before the arrival of the baby and today she felt ready to tackle every single one of them.

Already fully dressed, August placed Eleanor's morning cup of tea onto the bedside table and stood mesmerized by his beautiful wife. Her long golden curls seemed to have a life of their own; cascading across her forehead before resting on her shoulders, her full cheeks were radiant and her milky skin, flawless. "I don't want you overdoing it today Ellie!" he expressed, as all the while in his mind he was wondering if there would ever come a time when he wouldn't find his wife to be so captivating and when his heart wouldn't painfully ache with adoration for her.

"But, August, my darling, I feel so light and energetic this morning... whilst you're at work, I'm going to spring clean our room and sort through and arrange baby's layette, and when you return, I'd relish in a stroll along the river!"

"Today is the first day of August, my darling, and baby could arrive any day now! Remember what Doctor Thompson said...you mustn't tire yourself out but reserve your energy for when you'll need it most!"

"That's exactly why I'm so joyful today!" cried Eleanor, her bright eyes sparkling like jewels. "I love you so much, August and I adore everything about the month of August! It is and always will be my favourite month and I hope all of our future babies arrive in this month and when they are older and wish to marry, I shall insist that all weddings must take place in August!"

August burst into laughter, "Let's just concentrate on meeting our first baby, Ellie! You do say *the funniest of things* these days!"

"Well, I can't see anything at all comical in wanting to fill our home with children and just imagine if they should all be born in August! What a grand and delightful celebration we'd enjoy, every year!"

"My darling, Eleanor, you have filled my life with sweetness and my heart is brimming over with endless love for you, but for now I must be on my way before Austin starts tapping his foot upon the vestibule floor, as he does so often these days when I keep him waiting! Be sure to rest today, my love...write some letters, relax in the garden, but don't overdo it! Maybe I should have a word with Ma and Prudence! They would be more than willing to guard you all morning!"

"Fuss, fuss, fuss...don't fret my darling, I

promise I won't exhaust myself! Now come and kiss me goodbye!"

A lingering kiss made parting even more difficult. Eleanor wished for August's company on this day and he felt compelled to be close at hand until she had safely delivered their baby into the world, but knowing that it might still be weeks until that day, he dragged himself away from her softness, just as he heard Austin calling him from the vestibule.

As she sipped her tea, Eleanor gathered her thoughts and decided that August was, as usual quite right in his instructions and after preparing some lessons for master Charles, she would set about writing letters to Cynthia Thompson and Tilly. Although desperate to know how Tilly's romance was developing, Eleanor wrote with caution, careful not to put too much in a letter just in case it accidentally fell into the wrong hands; she didn't want anything to risk jeopardizing Tilly's chances, knowing how she'd fallen head over heels in love with Mr Ralph Berry. Every night Eleanor would pray that Tilly would find true love and enduring happiness; she'd suffered so much and risked her life during the weeks when she could have, so easily, declared how Rayne was holding the wrong woman captive. *Dear Tilly*, she mused, she was a true and loyal sister; the best.

Squealing with delight as she squeezed the piece

of dough between her chubby fingers, Felicity
was quite content to sit in her high chair in the
kitchen, just as long as she felt she had a hand in
assisting Rosa with the food preparation, it was
a new routine which had been adopted since
Tilly had been absent. Everyone made a habit of
constantly mentioning Tilly, not wanting Felicity
to forget about her special nanny, even though
she was now revelling in the extra attention she
received from Winifred and Prudence. Charles
was also extra attentive towards her, determined
to teach her the delights of digging the soil in
search of worms and the skill of ball throwing
and catching. At only eighteen months, Felicity
had become a most dominant member of the
household and had learned that by screaming at
the top of her voice she could usually get her
own way.

In his assumption that boys weren't in the habit
of constantly causing such a racket, Charles
prayed that Eleanor's baby would be a boy.

"I'm almost certain that your baby will be a boy,
Mrs Ellie!" he casually predicted, as Eleanor
placed the page of sums in front of him.

"And what makes you such an expert on
foreseeing the future, young Charles, pray tell?"

Charles chewed nervously on his bottom lip, as
Eleanor waited for his reply, "Well...I sort of
overheard my ma and Grandma Prudence
talking the other day and they said it!"

"*Master Charles!* How many times have you

found yourself in hot water from listening in on grown-up's conversations? You are too nosey by far!"

"*I'm not nosey!* Pa said that I'm just inquisitive which, he said, means that I'm intelligent!"

Eleanor suddenly winced as a sharp pain gripped her belly. She took a deep breath as she sat down, hoping that her indigestion wouldn't ruin her planned activities for the day.

"I don't expect *one* mistake today, Master Charles...and when you've completed the mathematic paper since today is the first day of August you are to compose a poem about this beautiful summer month!"

"Can't I write an essay instead, Mrs Ellie, I'm not very good at poems!"

"Then you must practise, in order to improve, Charlie!"

Leaving Charles long faced as he began his work, Eleanor was drawn to the tantalising aroma from the kitchen. Up to her elbows in flour and looking flushed, Rosa greeted Eleanor, whilst Felicity offered her a minute portion of her dough.

"Come and sit down, Ellie...I'm just about to take out the first batch of scones from the oven and the kettle has already boiled."

"*Then I will make the tea, Rosa!*"

"You need to sit down and rest, Ellie...I'll make the tea! I insist!"

Eleanor took in a deep breath and stared hard at

Rosa, "I know you mean well, Rosa, but I've only just risen from my bed and even if I look as though I need to rest this heavyweight, I'm full of energy and do not intend to sit down all day long! *I will make the tea!*"

"I'm sorry, Ellie, you must be quite vexed from everyone ordering you to put your feet up! I promise not to mention it again and would be most appreciative of a pot of tea made by your fair hands. I must quickly pop this loaf next door, I expect the ladies are waiting to eat their breakfast...unless you'd like to take it to them?"

"Oh no, Rosa, please tell them that I'm busy teaching Charles, I don't think I can face another dose of my grandmother's and mother in law's fussing at the moment. They've become like a pair of clucking hens! I will call on them this afternoon, with August!"

Rosa giggled, "Clucking hens! Then they will surely be glad of this loaf to peck at!"

Why don't you take Felicity to them, you'll be able to finish your chores in half the time, and be free to enjoy the beautiful weather!"

They both laughed out loud on viewing Felicity's ghostly appearance; she'd managed to reach the flour shaker and had been quite liberal with it.

"I'll take her later...don't want to scare the poor dears! *Felicity!* You are such a naughty girl!"

Felicity could only giggle and clap her hands together, causing clouds of flour to fill the kitchen.

\*\*\*\*\*\*\*\*\*\*\*\*

Feeling at home again as she walked along the familiar streets of Oxford, Tilly warned herself to put Ralph to the back of her mind. After her prolonged absence, she didn't want to meet Ellie with any trace of sadness upon her face and was sure that the moment she stepped over the threshold of the Hyde's home and was united with everyone again, her heart would cease to feel like a heavy, lead weight and her eyes might cease to well up every time she thought of Ralph. The scorching afternoon sun beat down upon her as she paused for a moment, in Hythe Bridge Street, to watch a family of ducks gliding gracefully upstream. How wonderful it must be to have your own family she mused, swallowing hard as she scolded herself for becoming emotional again. She knew that it would now be impossible to love another man as she loved Ralph and could now empathize with Rosa; she must have loved her beau with a similar passion. Nobody could take Ralph's place in her heart and she would likely remain a spinster forever.

\*\*\*\*\*\*\*\*\*\*\*\*

The searing pain which had inflicted Eleanor earlier that morning continued to surface every hour or two; she furtively wondered if it could be the beginning of her labour, but for the time being, kept it to herself. In her concealed excitement, however, she was finding it too difficult to concentrate on composing a letter and decided that in postponing them she might soon have some more exciting news to write about. She took tea beneath the shade of the apple trees and since Charles had exceeded in his poetry and answered every question on his mathematic paper correctly she allowed him to spend the afternoon in the garden, sketching plants and flowers. Feeling heavy-eyed in the balmy afternoon, Eleanor drifted off to sleep to the sound of chirping birds and the distant playful voices of local children but was suddenly awoken by a loud outcry from Rosa, her amplified voice reaching the garden. Charles, being his inquisitive self, immediately downed his pencil and rushed indoors. "He just can't help himself," thought Eleanor, out loud, with a smile upon her face. The pain had now moved to her lower back and was gradually intensifying. She felt comforted by the sound of August's voice in the distance, relieved that he'd returned home straight from his morning's work at Hyde &Son. There would be no writing for him this afternoon, she mused as another, more painful, cramp took her breath away.

He sounded loud and high spirited, and Rosa's voice was still audible too. There was definitely something going on inside, concluded Eleanor, as curiosity finally forced her to leave the comfort of her garden chair. But, as she cautiously eased her body up, a sudden gush of water left her standing in a small puddle. Wilma Hyde's words immediately sprung to mind and Eleanor knew that she wouldn't have long to wait until she became a mother.

Charles raced back into the garden, his cheeks flushed and his damp hair stuck to his sweaty forehead.

"*Mrs Ellie, Mrs Ellie!*" he cried, "Miss Tilly... "
His words were cut short as the appearance of August, Rosa and Tilly hurrying down the garden path, caused Eleanor to gasp and fall back down into her chair.

Unable to hold back a second longer, Tilly rushed toward her dearest friend and with tears streaming down both of their cheeks, their embrace lasted until another painful contraction caused Eleanor to cry out. The damp patch on Eleanor's pale blue dress had not gone unnoticed to Rosa, she whispered to August, advising him of how she believed he would very soon become a father and that she was going to fetch the midwife.

"Tilly!" sobbed Eleanor, "I never thought this day would come! I've missed you more than you could ever know!"

"Oh, believe me, Ellie, I *do* know, because life has been unbearable for me, without you!"

"My dearest Tilly, how wicked of me to be so thoughtless...you've been to Hell and back in order to safeguard me, and I will *never* in my entire life forget that!"

"You could never be thoughtless, Ellie! And at this moment I'd forgive you of anything because I know you are in pain and should be upstairs in bed! You've got a lot of hard work ahead of you my dear sister, and I'm going to be at your side throughout! Thank the Good Lord that I came home today to witness the arrival of my nephew or niece, into the world!"

Pale-faced and appearing gravely worried, August interrupted the reunion, "My darling, is it true? Are you feeling the pains of your condition?"

Tilly and Eleanor were unable to suppress their giggles as they glanced at each other,

"Oh! August! Please don't look so worried, this is a joyous occasion and what could make it better than having my dearest Tilly at my side? Wasn't it only this morning when I said to you how today felt as though it was going to be a special day?"

At five minutes past midnight, on the second of August, eighteen seventy-nine, the first cries a healthy baby boy filled the Hyde's home in Paradise Street, overwhelming his proud parents with an entirely new kind of love. Clarence Miller was perfect in every way and as his doting parents felt as though they could never fill their eyes enough with his miraculous sight, their attic room soon became overcrowded with everyone in awe of the new arrival. Prudence had never dreamt that she'd live to see her granddaughter again, but to survive to the day when she was able to cradle her great-grandson in her arms was nothing short of a miracle. Winifred was a grandmother at last and arrived with all the paraphernalia customary of grandmothers; enough beautifully embroidered nightgowns for baby Clarence's entire first year, a basket brimming over with tiny sized cardigans, hats, mittens and booties and for Eleanor, a cashmere shawl which Prudence and Winifred had shared the cost of, from one of Oxford's superior stores. Wilma and Austin presented the glowing parents with a silver rattle and a silver cup embossed with cute rabbits, and young master Charles who had not been able to sleep all night had gathered the largest bouquet from the garden shortly after August and Tilly had escorted Eleanor to her room. He was euphoric that Eleanor had delivered a boy, a new protégé for him to train in the skill of ball catching and bug hunting. Rosa's exquisite needlecraft skills had excelled and there were gasps of delight as Eleanor unwrapped the fine lace-trimmed, satin patchwork coverlet in pastel shades, each patch delicately embroidered with foliage and wildflowers.

# CHAPTER TWENTY-SEVEN

Following the birth of baby Clarence, the summer months seemed to rush past in a cloudy blur. Tilly's arrival couldn't have been better timed and once again she proved invaluable around the house and had soon returned to taking full care of Felicity, whose initial shyness had lasted for less than an hour. Charles was enjoying Tilly's more relaxed way of tutoring him while Eleanor, under Wilma's strict orders, was enjoying a six-week recuperating period and relishing in every precious minute spent with baby Clarence. Her heart was swollen with pure love for her firstborn; he was the light of her eyes and even during the difficult periods when he'd kept her awake throughout the entire night, she never tired of his demands.

"Come on Tilly let's take advantage of the last of the summer's sunshine before we have little choice than to remain at home all day long! I'm sure Prudence, Winifred and Rosa won't object to minding the children for an hour or two. We'll go for a stroll along the river!"

"Shouldn't we invite Rosa to join us? I'd hate for her to feel left out!"

"Oh Tilly, you must be the kindest and most thoughtful woman in England! But I've already mentioned my plans to her and she insisted that just we two go, besides, I don't feel that we've had a proper uninterrupted moment together since you came home. Young Clarence is so demanding and he's not even two months old!"

"Well alright then, you've persuaded me, but so long as we stay away from the stretch of river where we used to live and where you became so ill; I don't fancy reminiscing on those horrid times!"

"Oh, Tilly, you are funny! We won't go too far, maybe we could just sit under Hythe Bridge Street, and feed the ducks?"

"Yes, that sounds like a safe plan!" agreed Tilly, as she hurriedly cleaned away the mess which Felicity had managed to make whilst eating her luncheon.

"I shall remind Felicity of these days when she becomes a proper young Miss, with airs and graces...I didn't think it possible to cause such havoc with a bowl of soup and scrambled eggs!"

"Babies are certainly the messiest of creatures," giggled Eleanor.


A vacant bench beneath the shade of the ancient cobbled bridge proved the perfect place to take in the enchanting wildlife activities upon the river. The sweet fragrance from the overhanging wild climbing rose bush kissed the air and the calming sound of the river's gentle ripples produced a soothing, timeless atmosphere.

"This is such a beautiful little hideaway, Ellie! I wish the river had been so appealing when we were living on its banks!"

Eleanor smiled warmly, remembering the time when they'd sped through the open gates of the workhouse and ended up being forced to sleep on the river bank.

"I doubt this little spot is any less eerie in the dead of night, Tilly. We have certainly come a long way since those dismal days, haven't we!"

"Who would have thought that you would marry and become a mother so soon!"

"And you will too, my dearest Tilly, even if I have to drag August to Woolwich with me and instigate a little matchmaking, myself!" Appearing serious, all of a sudden, Tilly twisted her body, staring directly into Eleanor's eyes, "I know you mean well, Ellie and only want for me what you have yourself, the trait of a sincere sister, but Ralph Berry had a dozen or more opportunities to make his feelings known, so in conclusion that he clearly didn't want me to be a part of his life, I have resolved to dismiss him from my mind and in time, I pray that his image will be but a distant and vague memory in my heart."

"Are you absolutely certain, Tilly? Maybe he just needs a gentle push from an outsider to make him realise that he's made a huge mistake. I bet he's sat dreaming about you at this very moment and regretting not having acted upon his heart!"

A teardrop trickled down Tilly's flushed cheek; Eleanor could almost feel her sorrow and from experience knew the longing pain of estranged love. Thank God that August had harboured the same adoration for her as she had for him, otherwise, she would never have tasted true happiness again, she mused, as she allowed her emotions to give way to tears.

"Just look at us! We came out for a pleasant afternoon break and instead, we're sat here in tears!" choked Eleanor. "You deserve the best man, Tilly, and I'm quite sure that when the time is right whoever he might be, will sweep you off your feet!" Eleanor wrapped a comforting arm around Tilly's shoulder.

"From this moment forth, there will be no more mention of Mr Ralph Berry!" announced Eleanor, theatrically, "unless of course, *you* bring up the subject, Tilly!"

The sudden appearance of a flock of ducks about their ankles induced giggles.

"You always did have a way with the ducks, Tilly, they appear to adore and trust you!"

"And I just happen to have a shive of bread in my pocket too!" laughed Tilly, "which no doubt, they can smell!"

"*You see*! Now, why didn't I think to bring some food for the ducks?"

Staying clear of romance, the rest of their afternoon was spent chatting about the antics of young Clarence and Felicity and about how Charles was in a hurry for Clarence to grow up and join him in his pastimes. They spoke of the Hyde's ever-growing and prosperous business, glad that there was now a thriving ladies store too and that Rosa's talented skills were not being wasted. Her intricate embroidery had already provided her with a backlog of orders from some of Oxford's most influential women who desired unique and high-quality embroidery upon the bodices of their gowns. The tingling sensation in her breasts suddenly caused Eleanor to declare that Clarence was waiting for his feed and would be screaming the house down if they didn't make haste.

"It's like a miracle that you should know when baby Clarence is hungry!" expressed Tilly in awe. "I hope I experience such miracles one day if I should ever marry and have children."

"You will, Tilly, it's all part of that special bond between mother and child! And you *will* marry, there are no 'ifs' about it, and probably have a whole handful of babies, God willing! Oh, I hope Clarence hasn't disturbed August's afternoon of writing too much, he's already three weeks behind schedule with his latest book!"

Being the only man at home, in Paradise Street, August had been obliged to put down his pen and entertain the unexpected gentleman caller. Rosa was patiently trying to console Clarence, rocking him in her arms as she peered out of the front bedroom window in search of Eleanor and Tilly.

"Where on earth has your mamma got to, my little love? Doesn't she realise how irritated her poor boy is should he not receive his nourishment on demand?" Rosa brushed her lips across Clarence's forehead, he'd worked himself up into a sweaty state, and as much as Rosa tried to console him, it took little time before his hunger took precedence and he let out an even louder wail.

The gentleman caller had introduced himself as Mr Berry, informing August that it was he who had discovered Tilly when she'd been abandoned in a crate outside of his Woolwich home. He casually expressed how he'd been passing through Oxford and had decided to call in on Tilly, to inquire after her health. Sensing that Mr Berry was feeling awkward in his presence and that he was also hiding his real reasons for arriving in Paradise Street, August assured him that Tilly would soon be home, but got a distinct impression that his words only increased Mr Berry's nervous disposition. Rosa had delayed offering any hospitality, in the hope that Eleanor and Tilly would soon return and they could all take tea together.

Becoming overheated in his stylish tweed suit, Ralph felt uncomfortable as his damp shirt stuck to his skin, his collar felt unpleasantly tight and his palms were drenched. He hoped that August wasn't paying too much attention to his appearance, as the thought of leaving crossed his mind for the fourth time in the forty-five minutes that he'd been sat in the pristine drawing-room. He wondered how much Tilly had disclosed about her period spent in Antelope Street; did Mr Miller know more than he cared to mention in his light and friendly exchange of conversation? Had Tilly confessed her feelings for him to anyone other than her closest friend Ellie, he mused, as he dabbed the beads of sweat from his forehead.

"It is rather warm for September, is it not, Mr Berry?"

"Perhaps I will call another day, Mr Miller, I've already taken up too much of your valuable time!"

Leaving his seat to peer out of the window, August knew how angry Ellie would be if he allowed Ralph to leave before he'd spoken with Tilly. He'd heard endless reports from Ellie, about the blossoming romance which Ralph had seemed to shy away from, and instinct told him that Ralph's excessive nervousness was due to his intention to finally confess his love for Tilly.

"No, Mr Berry, I'm quite sure my wife and Tilly will not be delayed much longer...I will arrange for some refreshments for us...perhaps you'd care to sit in the garden where the air might prove more comfortable?"

Ralph glanced at his pocket watch, "Very well, Mr Miller, there *is* a later train to London; some refreshments in your garden would be greatly appreciated."

Now heavily laden with ripe fruit, the apple trees provided some much-needed shade; their leaves fluttered in the gentle breeze and the continuous baby's crying had now faded into the distance leaving Ralph feeling as though he could think again; he couldn't remember ever feeling so irritated by Cecil's wailing when he'd been an infant, but, he concluded, perhaps it was different when it was your own flesh and blood making such a ruckus.

Leaving Ralph seated at the wrought iron garden table and looking less flushed than he'd done since arriving in Paradise Street, August hurried back inside. Rosa insisted that she should prepare the cool lemonade and was glad to pass the hot and bothered, and extremely noisy baby into August's arms.

"I can't for the life of me think what could be keeping Eleanor! This is the first time she's ever been away from Clarence...I hope there's nothing amiss!"

"Don't worry so much, August, they're probably so indulged in conversation, that they've lost track of time!"

"Hmm, yes you females do love to chat! Poor Clarence, he's worked himself up into a dreadful state, couldn't we spoon feed him some of the milk from the pantry?"

"*Certainly not!* August!" stressed Rosa, in alarm,

"It would be sure to give poor, young Clarence a dreadful belly ache!"

# CHAPTER TWENTY-EIGHT

Just as August was about to carry the two glasses of lemonade out to the garden, Eleanor and Tilly could be heard chatting and giggling in the vestibule. With a shared glance of relief, August and Rosa hurried to meet them,
 "Oh, my darling boy!" cried Eleanor, as she viewed Clarence's red, screwed up face, his cries failing to cease even from the sight of his mother.
 "Thank God you're home!" exclaimed August as he hastily handed the noisy infant into Eleanor's arms.
 Rosa couldn't wait for a second longer to declare the news to Tilly, "There's a gentleman caller in the garden, Tilly, he's been here for ages waiting to see you!"
 A look of confusion caused Tilly's brow to wrinkle, "*For me?* But I don't know any gentlemen!"
 "I'm quite sure you are acquainted with this one!" chirped August, with a beaming smile.
 "It's Mr Berry!" declared Rosa.
Struggling to untie her tangled bonnet ribbons with one hand, Eleanor gasped at the mere mention of his name, feeling hopeful that this could be the start of a beautiful romance for Tilly. Clarence continued to scream.
 "I must take his little darling upstairs and settle

him, Tilly, but don't you dare let the infamous, Mr Berry leave until I return...I'm simply dying to meet the man who's captured your heart!"

Paying little attention to Eleanor's comments, Tilly's mind was already in a spin. Nervously licking her dry lips, she wondered what urgency could have brought Ralph Berry to Oxford.

"You'd best make haste, Tilly," advised August, "I don't think he has much time to spare before his return train departs!"

"Did he mention why he'd come to Oxford, August?"

"No, I don't recall him giving a precise reason...only that he was passing through and thought to enquire after you!"

"Oh, for heaven's sake, Tilly!" cried Rosa as she placed the tray carrying the jug of lemonade and two glasses into her hands. "Go and see for yourself! The poor man is positively parched and has been waiting for over an hour for you!"

The sight of Tilly making her way towards him took Ralph's breath away; spontaneously rising from his chair, he felt his heart melt and was already feeling tongue-tied. He warned himself to allow his heart to speak freely in her presence as his eyes fixed on her delicate frame. She was even more beautiful than he remembered, she looked the picture of health and her flawless skin appeared as smooth as silk.

"Tilly!" he declared. "It's so wonderful to see you

again! How are you?" Barely taking his eyes off her, he took the tray from her hands and placed it on the table. Tilly looked into his misty eyes, as she felt her heart contract. The pain of loving him was like a sore, open wound and she prayed that his presence was because he harboured the same feelings of love for her; she couldn't bear to be left broken-hearted again.

"I'm very well, Ralph, how are you and how is your dear mother and young Cecil?"

"Oh, Tilly, I've missed you so much! I have been but half a man without you and have been the biggest fool to have let you out of my life! Can you ever forgive me, *my darling Tilly?*"

Like two links from a broken chain they both, instinctively, took a step towards each other and within seconds were locked in an embrace that would seal their love forever. Tilly's tears brimmed over and Ralph found himself watery-eyed as his heart pounded loudly.

"I've been such a foolish man, Tilly! I don't know why I failed to voice my true feelings for you weeks ago when our parting wrenched my heart from its place of tranquillity. I love you, Tilly! Please make me whole again and agree to become my wife! Marry me, my darling! I beg of you!"

Tilly was unable to speak as her painful throat tensed; still wrapped in Ralph's arms, she nodded her head, her teary eyes clouding her vision as she looked up at Ralph's handsome face. She nodded her head again and spluttered out her words, "Ralph, *my dearest Ralph*...There is nothing which would please me more, my darling!"

"I love you so much my Tilly, *my girl from the wooden crate!* Cecil's words were ringing with truth when he spoke of a treasure being left outside of our front door. I was just *too* stubborn to admit to it, though, and was determined to punish myself by closing my heart forever! You are my special treasure, Tilly and I have been an absolute halfwit to let you slip away... risking our love to be blown away upon the summer's breeze! I cannot live without you, my precious love, and by accepting my marriage proposal you have restored the gaping void in my heart. "*Oh Ralph*, I never thought this day would come; I have loved you since the day of our first encounter! Why it was only this very afternoon, I confessed to Ellie that since you were gone from my life, I would be resolved to a life without the love of a husband...*A spinster's life*, in fact!"

"My sweet, brave Tilly, let's not wait a moment longer, let's make the arrangements for our wedding to take place as soon as possible...we've wasted too much time already, my love!"

"I do have one condition, though, Ralph!" stated Tilly, seriously.

Ralph tilted his head, as he gazed lovingly into Tilly's misty eyes, "Anything for you my darling!"

"That you don't make a habit of referring to me as *the girl from the wooden crate!*"

Their serious faces suddenly melted as they laughed with sheer delight, falling into each other's arms again, and finding each other's lips. Accompanied by the enchanting chorus from the early evening chaffinches and blackbirds, a sweet, lingering first kiss, beneath the shade of the apple tree would be an unforgettable memory which they'd keep in their hearts forever.

As the glowing September sun began to set, one by one Tilly's adoring adopted family arrived into the garden. Clarence was now sleeping contentedly in Eleanor's arms, Rosa had prepared a spread to be enjoyed in the pleasantly cool evening, and Wilma and Austin were as thrilled as Tilly that at last, she had found her true love.

"August! You should write another love story, about Tilly and Ralph," suggested Wilma. "Your debut novel was an absolute delight, and I haven't yet met an acquaintance who hasn't thoroughly enjoyed it and who would be thrilled to read another such similar novel!"

August lovingly stroked Clarence's cheek, "No, Mrs Hyde, *'Searching for Eleanor'* was guided and influenced by my heart...I doubt I will ever write another love story again...my heart is content and I am the happiest man alive...It's detective novels only from now on!"

"Actually!" Raph intervened. "It is I who is the happiest man alive! Especially since my dear Tilly has agreed to marry me!"

Gasps of delight and words of congratulations overwhelmed the garden, just as Prudence and Winifred arrived with Felicity.

"We weren't informed of any party going on today!" expressed Winifred, annoyingly, with her eyes firmly fixed on Ralph.

"We are celebrating the engagement of Tilly and Mr Berry!" declared Austin, "and believe me, ladies, this celebratory party is as much a surprise to all of us, as it is to you!"

The evening turned into an extended and joyful party, and with Ralph having missed his last train back to London, he stayed the night with Prudence and Winifred, who were already buzzing with plans and ideas for the forthcoming wedding. Tilly, Eleanor and August already knew that poor Ralph would get little sleep, but were all far too excited themselves to give it more than a single thought of concern.

"If Ralph is to be joining our family, he'll have to get used to my mother's and your grandmother's eccentric ways!" voiced August.

"Oh, August! It's only just crossed my mind!" expressed Eleanor, her voice suddenly taking on a sad tone. "If Tilly is to marry Ralph, she will surely be leaving Oxford to reside in London!

After all, Ralph's work and family are there!" Comforting his sad-faced wife, August spoke quietly in her ear, "Don't let Tilly see you looking so downcast, my darling...look at her, I've never before witnessed her so high spirited and jubilant! You've managed without her by your side before and at least this time, you will be assured that she's happy and living a fulfilling life, and besides, London is only a stone's throw away and the railway is improving  and becoming faster with every passing year!"

"You're right, of course, August. After everything she's been through, Tilly deserves her share of happiness more than most and I shouldn't be selfish...but I will miss her so much and I know she will miss her family, here in Oxford too!"

"That's life, my darling...love doesn't always come without its sacrifices, but we'll soon become accustomed to the new ways, you'll see."

"I know, August, I consider myself fortunate to even *have* such a wonderful sister as Tilly, and I'm truly consumed with joy for her! Love will overcome the distance between us; after all, isn't it often said, how love conquers all!"

"And never a truer statement spoken, my darling!" agreed August.

# EPILOGUE

It was during the last week of October when Tilly and Ralph became man and wife, just two days prior to Eleanor and August's second wedding anniversary. Held in Ralph's local church which was overflowing with guests, the entire celebration turned out to be a far grander and noisier celebration than Eleanor's wedding and was attended by over a hundred guests. Coming from a well established and popular family, the folk of Woolwich were delighted that, at last, Ralph Berry had found happiness again after so many turbulent years and after proving to be a doting father to his motherless son. They were eager to celebrate his happiness and to convey their approval of the nuptial between Tilly and one of the most respected and adored gentlemen of Woolwich. Everyone from Paradise Street, including Winifred and Prudence, had insisted on making the journey to London to attend Tilly's wedding; they were the only family she had, and with Eleanor's first-hand experience of the pain of such a special day taking place without the presence of proud parents, it was all the more important to show the many guests of the groom's family that she belonged and was thoroughly cherished by her own, slightly unconventional, and adoring family from Oxford.

Adorned in her lavish wedding gown, Tilly appeared a picture of beauty and stunned everyone in the congregation as she glided like a graceful swan up the aisle. Created by Wilma and Rosa and with Prudence and Winifred working tirelessly on the train, the work of art was a shimmering, ivory silk taffeta ensemble, with embroidered pastel pink rose buds to the bodice and seed pearls covering the leg of mutton sleeves. The many-layered skirts, which took on the shape of a bell were trimmed with Chantilly lace, as was the extensive train.

The disclosure of a happy, but well-kept secret was announced by Ruth Berry towards the end of the wedding breakfast. Mr Page, who had been waiting patiently for many years for Ruth to be free of her family obligations, had asked her to marry him as soon as he'd heard of Ralph's intentions to marry Tilly. They had kept it to themselves, even though Ruth was bubbling over with the joy of beginning her very own new adventure. It was music to Ralph's ears, who had worried that his new married life would prove difficult, in the long run, with him being torn between his wife and mother and with the possibility that his mother might feel left out after all the years of living with him and Cecil under their roof. It also meant that the clandestine offer from Mr Hyde would now become quite viable, although Ralph decided to keep that to himself until after his mother's wedding and when he was assured of her happiness and that she'd be in agreement with him taking Cecil away from daily life.

Tilly's wedding was an overwhelmingly dreamy occasion that sprouted new blooms of love and romance. Ruth Berry wasn't the only woman to be walking upon clouds that day, and when Tilly had introduced Rosa to the American born, physician who had been so meticulous in his care for her during her initial days in Woolwich, it was blatantly obvious how he was instantly drawn to Rosa and spent most of the evening conversing with her and making sure her plate and cup were always full. Doctor Fairweather's attentiveness had not failed to catch Wilma's eye, who furtively passed comment to Eleanor of her opinion that they would soon be organising another wedding breakfast. Eleanor prayed it would be the case, nothing could be more pleasing to her than to witness Rosa finding love and a decent husband.

"He is rather dashing don't you agree, Wilma!" whispered Eleanor as they watched the couple engrossed in conversation.

"He certainly is, Ellie, and what's more, Oxford would welcome such a talented Doctor!"

Eleanor laughed out loud, "Oh, Mrs Hyde, I do love your determination in trying to keep us workers, close to hand!"

Shocked by, Eleanor's words, Wilma took hold of her arm and was exceptionally serious in her reply, "Please don't *ever* give yourself or Tilly and Rosa that inappropriate title, Eleanor! In mine and Austin's eyes, you are all part of our much-adored family and we love and cherish you all in the same way as we do Charles and Felicity! which reminds me, that someone must take Charles away from the food, every time I glance at him he is filling his greedy mouth! It's most embarrassing!"

Warmed by Wilma's declaration on such an emotional day, Eleanor fought back her tears of joy. "Don't worry, Wilma, I'll distract him; it's about time he got to know, young Cecil Berry! I have a feeling that they might find themselves as close as brothers one day!"

*"Has Austin been talking to you?"*

"He didn't need to, Mrs Hyde!" giggled Eleanor, "he's been in cahoots with Ralph throughout the day! My husband's detective brain must be rubbing off on me!"

"Either that or young Charles's inquisitiveness is proving contagious!" joked Wilma, smiling broadly.


Beginning her married life in the familiar cottage in Antelope Street and having young Cecil at her side, helped to make Tilly's longing for Felicity, Charles and baby Clarence a little more bearable. Cecil was as overjoyed to have a new mother as Ralph was to have a new wife, and within a fortnight, with Tilly's permission, he began calling her Ma. It was eight weeks later, that Ruth Berry become the new Mrs Page and moved into the ample, but rather overheated, rooms above Mr Page's, forge. It felt peculiar to Tilly at first but she quickly revelled in being the lady of the house and set about making a few adjustments to the place, putting her personality into the decor and soft furnishings and rearranging the layout of the furniture, impressing Ralph with the new modern look. There wasn't a week which passed by that Eleanor and Tilly didn't correspond with each other; they were both missing each other more than anyone could possibly understand and Tilly often found herself in tears when she remembered the terrible years which she and Eleanor had suffered during their years in the workhouse, it was a period which both young women tried to put to the back of their minds, but now and again the pain of the past somehow found itself floating to the surface. On more exciting and optimistic news, they discussed the growing romance between Doctor George Fairweather and Rosa. The besotted doctor had, apparently, already attended an interview at the Radcliffe infirmary, and was awaiting news of its outcome. Unanimously, Eleanor and Tilly wrote how they strongly considered that should he be accepted for the new position, he should waste no more time and proceed with his proposal of marriage to Rosa.

Hyde&Son had expanded further and now boasted its very own bridal department. Tilly was euphoric to discover she was with child with her confinement due around the time of her first wedding anniversary. The letter to Eleanor about her happy news had cross paths with Eleanor's letter, in which she also wrote of how she was with child again. The news made Eleanor even more determined to persuade Austin to take on Ralph at Hyde&Son sooner than had already been discussed; Eleanor could think of nothing sweeter than for her and Tilly to share the ups and downs of their coming months of confinement. Between them, and with the help of their powers of persuasion, within a month, Ralph had left his employment with the Woolwich tailor and the family were excitedly anticipating the beginning of a new life in Oxford. Having already taken a clandestine journey into Oxford, Ralph had viewed a couple of potential houses to move his family into, one of which was close to Paradise Street. By the summer of eighteen eighty, Tilly and Eleanor were once again united, and both three months away from their confinement. They couldn't get enough of each other's company, and with Tilly spending more time in the Hyde's home than the cottage which Ralph had rented out for them, Austin came up with the idea of converting the attic and the top floor of Winifred's and Prudence's home into a similar living space as August and Eleanor occupied next door. In the few weeks in which he'd worked at Hyde&Son, Ralph proved to be an invaluable asset; he was far more knowledgeable when it came to the latest in men's fashion and was a convincing salesman.

The glorious, extended summer throughout September made for the perfect wedding day for Rosa and Doctor George Fairweather; it saw the end of Rosa's days working and often living in Paradise Street, as her new married life to a prominent American surgeon meant that she would be residing in a fashionable Oxford townhouse, close to Oxford's Radcliffe Infirmary.

Cecil and Charles had become inseparable, becoming lifelong friends, even though their later education took them along completely different paths. Following in his father's footsteps, Cecil became a tailor and worked alongside Ralph in Hyde&Son, and when Wilma and Austin eventually retired, in eighteen ninety Ralph invested all his savings into a share of the ever-growing clothing empire and it was renamed, *Berry, Hyde&Sons*. Charles went on to become a prominent Oxford lawyer and Clarence, although taking a long while to decide where his passions lay, worked in various jobs until realising how he yearned to live and work away from the increasingly busy City. He had just turned twenty-five when, with a little financial help from his proud parents, he purchased a modest farm close to East Hanwell. Sadly both Winifred and Prudence had passed away by this time. Winifred had been taken first, after a severe bout of winter bronchitis, which even Prudence's special remedies had failed to cure. Prudence never recovered from the loss of Winifred; they had spent so many of their twilight years together and since Winifred's departure, Prudence appeared to lose her determined attitude towards life, even though everyone made an extra effort to rally around her in a bid to make up for the huge void which had overwhelmed her existence. When she became feverish the following year, it was as though she had lost her will to fight, and yearned to join her dearest companion in the Hereafter.

Tilly's firstborn was a beautiful baby girl, born a week before Eleanor delivered a brother for Clarence, who was the image of his brother and was named Theodore. Tilly went on to have two more children, all girls and all named after flowers; Primrose, Lily and Marigold. Ralph called them his blooms from heaven, delighted that all three took after their beautiful mother in appearance.

In Whitechapel, Tommy Kettle had never quite
got over his love for Rayne and found it hard to
ever trust another woman. He turned his back
on romance and had become Buster Forbes'
right-hand man in the setting up and running of
a brand new music hall, a more refined
establishment than before, with only the best
entertainers which Whitechapel had to offer
being employed upon its stage. Buster continued
with his illegal sideline in underhand dealings,
until the day when his heart was captured by
Henrietta McBride, a forty-eight-year-old,
wealthy opera singer who had been persuaded
by Tommy to take the starring role at the music
hall for one week only in order to attract
customers from every corner of Whitechapel and
beyond. There had been an instant attraction
between the rather large framed, flamboyant
Miss McBride and Buster Forbes, a match which
nobody could ever have imagined would be a
success. They were married shortly after their
whirlwind romance with Henrietta putting an
end to Buster's contraband runs, terrified that he
might become the next victim of the gallows. She
was besotted with him and showered him with
the wealth she'd been putting aside throughout
her singing career. Buster became a tame and
kept man, living every day of his life in luxury,

and mingling with the fashionable operatic set of the West End.

Tommy was left solely in charge of the music hall, and given a far larger percentage of the takings. Within a year, he had become one of Whitechapel's most eligible and wealthiest bachelors, with a trail of young maidens pursuing his assets.

Never recovering from his broken heart or finding a woman who measured up to Rayne, Tommy Kettle lived his entire life as a bachelor, even though his rise in status gave him the opportunity of being able to pick and choose from dozens of pretty women. He passed away in his prime after a short illness leaving his sister's to benefit from his healthy bank balance.

The small fortune which Sid Crewe had stolen from Peggy's grocery was soon gambled away and wasted on liquor. Sid had relished in his few weeks of being an imposter in the social circles of the wealthier folk, who had seen straight through him, but the 'Scavenger' had accumulated more enemies than friends throughout his life and it failed to shock anyone in the East End when his beaten-up body was washed ashore on the filthy banks of the Thames. He was neither missed nor mourned but laid to rest in a paupers burial ground with only the clergymen in attendance.

Rayne Jackson returned to England after eleven years, shortly after Elizabeth Jackson had passed away after a long and crippling illness. Rayne, who had refused every suitor who'd attempted to woo her had spent her final three years in Bombay, nursing her mother and had booked her passage home as soon as her mother had drawn her last breath. Elizabeth had left a tidy sum behind her, having inherited the entire estate from her companion who'd died from a poisonous snake bite after only two years of living in India. Being a woman of a stubborn nature, she had refused to heed to the local's advice of not bathing in the nearby, scenic and tranquil lagoon which was notorious for its lethal snakes. She foolishly believed her wealthy status would protect her from such dangers. Now a wealthy woman approaching thirty Rayne purchased a peaceful country cottage in Durham, far away from London, which held too many upsetting memories for her to cope with and which was a City she vowed never to set foot in again. Convinced that she'd never again love a man as she'd loved August Miller, she lived a life of make-believe, in the pretence that she had actually married August and that it was he and not her mother who'd passed. She wore the engraved bracelet, still persuading herself that it was a gift from August. To anyone who happened to inquire about her personal life, she would state how she was in mourning for her beloved late husband. She lived the life of a recluse, not even employing a maid or a cook, and she was soon viewed as an eccentric, slightly unhinged woman, and one to be avoided. The sound of her fiddle could often be heard by passers-by, as the sad melodies wafted out of the open windows of her lonely home.

Paradise Street, 1931

"Oh August, I'm feeling so old and weary tonight and my eyes are tired and sore!" complained Eleanor in despair.

August sat up in bed and turned on the bedside lamp, " How many times must I tell you, my darling, you do too much...tomorrow we will picnic in the garden and spend the entire day being lazy! It's not a crime to be lazy at our age you know!"

Eleanor looked lovingly at August, she loved him more than she'd ever imagined it was possible to love someone. Beneath his ageing face and unruly whiskers, she could still see the young man who'd entered her heart so unexpectedly when she was just a young girl of fourteen. He was her life, her dearest friend and her most treasured love.

"You're right as always my darling husband. Did I ever tell you how much I love you?"

"Once or twice, my sweetheart! Did I ever tell you how you have made my life richer than that of the richest king and that I love you more than my tongue knows how to express!"

"Hmmm, you might have done!" giggled Eleanor.

"You still have the same enchanting giggle that you had fifty-seven years ago, my darling!"

"Oh August, you've made me feel even older now with your mention of all those years which have passed by so speedily! Why does life suddenly catch up with you like a thief in the night, stealing away your youth! Where *have* all those years gone? I detest old age and it's only when I look into the mirror when I realise how old and decrepit I am!"

"Enough of that talk, now Eleanor, you'll feel ten years younger after a good night's sleep, and remember, I'm six years older than you!"

"We've had a fulfilling life together though, haven't we, August, darling?"

"The best, my love; the very best!"

"I do so very often find myself thinking about poor Rosa and George! What made them decide to visit New York after all the years in which George had been away? I often wonder!"

"Fate, my darling!"

Eleanor allowed her tears to roll off her face and drip onto the bedsheets, "I suppose it was a blessing that they didn't have children, even though I prayed and wished it for them for so many years. When I think of all the lives wasted on the Titanic, those young folk, who'd barely began their lives...."

"There, there, my sweetheart put those thoughts out of your mind, otherwise you'll never sleep, and we're going on a picnic tomorrow, remember, and I don't want my wife looking weary!"

"Read to me, August...*please.*"

"Very well, my love, what would you like to hear? How about a chapter from one of Theodore's novels, he really does have a unique and appealing style!"

"He certainly takes after his dear father, but I think I'd prefer a chapter from one of your books, my darling ...*Searching For Eleanor*, please."

August rolled his eyes, as he smiled lovingly at Eleanor, "I'm surprised you don't know every chapter of that book by heart!"

"Perhaps I do, but I simply wish to hear my adorable husband's voice! I love you, August Miller! "

"And I love you too, my sweet, Eleanor Miller!"

Printed in Great Britain
by Amazon

78614647R00159